DESPERATE
MEASURES

Visit us at www.boldstrokesbooks.com

By the Author

From This Moment On

True Confessions

Missing

Trusting Tomorrow

Desperate Measures

DESPERATE MEASURES

by
PJ Trebelhorn

2014

CREDITS
EDITOR: CINDY CRESAP
PRODUCTION DESIGN: SUSAN RAMUNDO
COVER DESIGN BY SHERI (GRAPHICARTIST2020@HOTMAIL.COM)

Acknowledgments

Thanks once again to Len Barot and everyone behind the scenes at Bold Strokes Books. I couldn't imagine working with a better group of people.

Cindy Cresap, thank you, thank you, thank you. You've taught me some very valuable things. I just hope I can remember it all.

Sheri—Thanks for another awesome cover! You're the best!

Thanks to my sister, Carol Trebelhorn, for being my biggest cheerleader. You mean the world to me.

Susan and Harvey Campbell, thank you for being the best people I've ever had the pleasure of knowing. And for asking me "how's the writing going?" every time I see you. You keep me on my toes.

Hugh and Betty James, thank you for making me feel like part of the family. I don't think I could ever put into words how much you both mean to me.

Dedication

For Cheryl,
You are my rock

CHAPTER ONE

Kay Griffith sat back in her chair with an audible sigh, steadfastly refusing to admit defeat. She knew she was being hardheaded, but she *really* hated to lose—hated it with a passion, as a matter of fact. She raised her eyes back up to the computer screen and shook her head.

"Computer kicking your ass again?" she heard her partner, Larry Quinn, ask from behind her. He chuckled, and she glared at him as he took a seat at his own desk, facing hers. She tossed a paper clip at him, which he caught and immediately sent back in her direction. "You should stop playing those damn solitaire games, Griff. They program the freaking thing so it beats you more often than not."

"I know that," she said before exiting the game. She was about to ask him if he wanted a cup of coffee when his phone rang. "What are the chances it might be Janice with our lab results?"

"Quinn," he said when he snatched up the phone and held it to his ear. He held Kay's gaze as he listened. "We'll be right there."

"What?" Kay asked before he even had a chance to hang up. She grabbed her keys from the desk as Quinn headed for the elevator.

"The Jane Doe in a rape case woke up a few minutes ago." He pushed the button to call the elevator and then turned back to look at her, a smile on his face. "She says she got a look at his face, *and* she knew her attacker."

"We're homicide, Quinn, not vice." Kay started to head back to her desk, unable to hide her annoyance. Waiting for Janice from forensics to call with lab results would be more productive than talking to a rape victim. They needed to prove Tommy Rayne had killed their victims, and it was all she cared about right now.

"Matthews from vice is with the rape victim, and she thinks we'll want to hear what this woman has to say. What can it hurt? It has to beat sitting around here picking our noses while we wait for the lab to call."

Kay nodded. If Matthews thought it was something they needed to hear, then who was she to argue? Janice had both their cell phone numbers anyway.

Kay smiled amiably at the nurse who was just coming out of Jane Doe's room as they approached. The nurse stopped in front of them when she saw where Kay and Quinn were headed.

"No visitors," she said with a quick shake of her head.

Kay pulled her detective's badge out to show the nurse. She looked back and forth between them before finally stepping aside and muttering under her breath as she headed back toward the nurse's station.

"Don't think she's very happy to see us." Quinn chuckled as he spoke quietly enough for only Kay to be able to hear him.

"Not our problem." Kay shrugged but didn't look back as she opened the door and entered the hospital room. Polite greetings were made between the two sets of detectives before Kay got down to business. The woman lying in the bed was unrecognizable due to the beating she'd suffered at the hands of her rapist. Kay forced down the bile she felt rising in her throat and concentrated on what had to be done. "What do we have here, Amy?"

"Her name is Tina Carson, thirty-two years old, works as a waitress in the greasy spoon down on Third." Detective Amy Matthews glanced at her notes, and Kay watched her expectantly. Amy had gone through the academy with Kay, but they'd drifted apart when Amy was assigned to vice while Kay opted for homicide. Amy looked up from her notes, her professional demeanor faltering slightly. "He beat the hell out of her, Griff."

"I can see that," Kay said. Amy looked as though she was about to break down, and Kay felt bad for her old friend. She glanced at Quinn, and without saying a word, he knew what she wanted. He gestured for Amy's partner to join him out in the hallway. When the two men were gone, Kay urged Amy to take a seat, and then she knelt in front of her, a hand resting gently on Amy's knee. "Why didn't you move to homicide with me? I know we see some brutal things there, but at least we don't have to deal with the pain these victims go through during their recovery. You weren't cut out for this, Amy."

"This is why I joined the force, Kay. You know that."

Kay stood slowly and turned to look at the woman who appeared to be unconscious in the bed. Kay admitted to herself she would never be able to do the job Amy had taken on. It was extremely heartrending to see the violent aftermath of some sick fuck's idea of a good time. In Kay's opinion, it was much easier to deal with death than the brutal results of a beating. At least if the victims were dead, they weren't in pain.

"Why were we called in for this, Amy?" Kay asked, finally turning back to her. She thought she knew why, but she wanted to hear the words spoken out loud. On the ride to the hospital, she and Quinn concluded that the only reason Matthews would want them there would be if the man this woman was accusing of raping her was Tommy Rayne. She hoped they were right. "There wasn't a homicide in this case, was there?"

Amy quickly pulled herself together and stood as she brusquely wiped the tears from her face. She managed a slight smile as she walked over to stand next to Kay.

"Tommy Rayne is your primary suspect in those prostitution murders, right?"

"Yeah." Kay smiled inwardly, allowing herself a moment of fantasizing what it might be like to finally take the fucker down.

"She fingered him."

"By name?" Kay asked, unable to mask her surprise. The best she and Quinn hoped for was a description that matched Rayne. If she'd been able to give Amy the guy's name, then it was even better.

"It seems he's a regular at the diner." Amy put her notebook back in her pocket and stood with her arms crossed. She never took her eyes from the victim's face while she spoke. "Tina said she was always a little bit spooked by him, and who wouldn't be? He's the scariest looking guy I've ever seen. Anyway, she evidently didn't think anything of it when he was waiting outside the diner the other night when she got off work. He offered to walk her to her car, but she refused. She says he wasn't too pleased about her response, and he grabbed her. He pulled her down the alley to where his car was parked and then he drove to the park where she was found the next morning."

"She said it was Tommy Rayne?" Kay asked, not sure she was understanding correctly because the pulse was pounding so loudly in her ears. This would make things so much easier on her and Quinn. But her skepticism quickly kicked in. In her experience, if something seemed too good to be true, then it usually was. "She actually said his name?"

"Yes. She told me Tommy Rayne did this to her."

"You're the best, Amy." Kay grabbed her and turned her before giving her a big kiss on the cheek. She smiled at the blush creeping up Amy's neck and cheeks. "I'm sorry. I just couldn't help myself."

"Not a problem." Amy smiled and looked away from Kay and back to Tina's battered body. "Let me know if I can do anything to help with your case. I want him to go down for this just as much as you and Quinn do."

"I will." Kay put a hand on her arm and waited for Amy to meet her eyes. "We'll probably want to question her—if for no other reason than to hear her say the bastard's name. You have enough to get a warrant for his arrest, but I need to know she'll be willing to testify in court. When you called Quinn, you said she was awake."

"I'll do what I can to convince her. They gave her a sedative before you got here because she was in a lot of pain. She probably won't wake again until morning, but I'll give you a call as soon as she does."

"I appreciate it." Kay nodded and let go of her arm. "You should get some rest. You look tired."

"This job isn't exactly conducive to sleeping well, Kay." She smiled wanly and shook her head. "When I do manage to fall asleep, I generally have nightmares."

"If you ever want to talk, you have my number."

"Kay." Amy's voice stopped Kay on her way to the door. Kay turned to face her. "How about getting together for a drink sometime?"

"You aren't asking me out on a date, are you?" Kay smiled and took an awkward step toward her. It was a silly question because she knew Amy was a year into her relationship with their forensics guru, Janice Green. But then again, Amy had never kept her attraction to Kay a secret.

"No, I'm not, but even if I were, you can't tell me you're straight like you did when we were in the academy."

Amy had laid her heart on her sleeve the night she confessed her growing feelings for Kay. But Kay hadn't been ready to admit she was gay at the time. Her parents had instilled in her and her brother how being gay was a sin, and all sinners went to hell. It was all Kay had been able to think of the night Amy opened up to her, even though Kay knew deep down her feelings toward women were much more than platonic.

"Yes, I did tell you that, didn't I?" Kay had finally come out when she turned twenty-four, but they'd never made an attempt to date. They'd both agreed they had too good of a friendship to screw things up by sleeping together.

"I just miss being friends with you," Amy said.

"I'll give you a call sometime," Kay said, knowing she probably never would. She'd never really been convinced Amy would be satisfied with just friendship between them, and Kay would never even think about being the *other woman*. They nodded at each other before Kay left the room.

Chapter Two

Q uinn, Griffith, my office now," Lieutenant Paul Webber
bellowed from across the room.

"Shit," Quinn muttered as he met Kay next to her desk.
"This can't be good."

They entered his office, and Kay shut the door behind her
before she and Quinn took the chairs in front of the desk. Paul
was sitting behind the desk, staring rather intently at his hands,
which were palms down in front of him. Kay had a bad feeling
about this meeting. Everyone was silent, waiting for Paul to
speak first.

"Rayne was released this morning," he finally said.

Kay did her best to keep her temper under control, but she
could feel her blood pressure rising steadily. She gripped the arms
of her chair as she leaned forward, and even Quinn's steadying
hand on her forearm didn't help to calm her.

"What the fuck do you mean *he was released?*" She spoke
through gritted teeth. This job was beginning to grate on her
nerves. They did everything by the book, and it still seemed like
they couldn't get the bad guys off the streets for more than a few
days at a time.

"Griff…" Quinn warned her quietly.

"He's got a lawyer who knows how to work the system,"
Paul answered, obviously ignoring her choice of words. He

wasn't one to put up with anyone who spoke to him in such a manner, but he'd always had a soft spot for Kay, and she took advantage without even realizing it sometimes. "And we don't have a victim who's willing to testify anymore."

"What do you mean?" Kay was livid. She began to pace in the cramped area behind the chairs. "I spoke with Tina myself. She said she wanted nothing more than to get that bastard off the streets."

"I guess she had a change of heart," Paul answered calmly. "She found out he's our prime suspect for two brutal murders. That, along with the fact he supposedly threatened her life before leaving her naked in the park, has made her rethink her agreement to testify. Without her, there was nothing to hold him on. She claims she was mistaken about who raped her. She's now refusing to press charges."

"Fuck!" Kay stormed out of the office and went straight to her desk to grab her car keys. Her volatile temper was legendary around the squad room, and no one even bothered to look in her direction. Before she could make it to the elevator, Quinn was at her side.

"Griff, where are you going?"

"I'm going to pay Tommy Rayne a visit." Quinn grabbed her arm, but she pulled away from him. "Just leave it alone, Quinn. I need to see him. I need to let him know we're watching him. All it's going to take is one wrong move on his part, and he'll be back in jail."

"Fine, but I'm going with you."

"I can do this myself. I don't need a babysitter."

"Hell, I'm not going because I'm worried about you, Griff." He grinned at her as he shrugged and motioned for her to get in the elevator. "I know you can take care of yourself. I'm worried about what he'll end up looking like if he pisses you off any more than you already are."

She loved Quinn like a brother. In fact, she loved Quinn more than her own brother. He was always there for her, looking out for her even when she thought she didn't need taking care of. She wondered now, as she often did, why some woman hadn't snatched him up. He was going to make one hell of a husband and father someday.

❖

Kay grimaced when they walked into the pawnshop. The place smelled like someone had left the garbage sitting out for about a month. She didn't even spare the rest of the establishment a glance but headed straight for the counter in back. She didn't need to look around, because every seedy corner of the place was burned into her brain. Unfortunately, Rayne's shop looked nothing like the places she kept seeing pop up on those idiotic television reality shows. Rayne certainly didn't have the crowds coming into his store that they did either. He preferred to cater to the criminal clientele.

"Tommy Rayne. Now," Kay said, and the young man working behind the counter jumped at the forceful command. His eyes darted nervously back and forth between Kay and Quinn as they both held up their badges for him to see, but he shook his head.

"He's not here," he said, unable to keep his voice steady. Kay took a good look at him and tried to calm herself down. He couldn't have been more than seventeen years old. The tag he wore on his shirt gave Kay his name.

"Maybe you didn't understand me, Billy." Kay shrugged off Quinn's hand, which had gone to her forearm. She leaned forward and resisted the urge to grab the kid by the shirtfront. "I want to see Tommy Rayne, and I want to see him now. I'm not leaving until he comes out here and talks to me. So you're either going to get off your ass and tell him we're here, or else get on the phone and tell him he needs to get here yesterday, because I'm guessing two detectives taking up residence in his store isn't going to be too good for business."

The kid looked at Quinn for help, but he shrugged as he spoke. "I suggest you do as the lady says. She's not in a very good mood this morning."

Billy disappeared into the back of the store, and Kay finally felt herself relax just a bit. She turned and glared at Quinn.

"What the fuck was that?"

"What?" he asked as he took a step back. "I was playing good cop to your bad. Isn't that our usual way of doing things?"

Kay chuckled and shook her head. Who in their right mind would believe she was the more ill-tempered of the two? Quinn was a good five inches taller than her five feet ten, and weighed well over a hundred pounds more than she did. To look at the two of them, there was no doubt which cop a suspect would look at to be more sympathetic, which was precisely why their act was so convincing. Especially to young kids like the one she'd just strong-armed.

"Maybe you two good detectives haven't heard," Tommy Rayne said as he approached them from behind. Kay turned to face him. "I was released because your so-called *victim* recanted her statement."

"Oh, we heard," Kay managed in a voice that was calmer than she felt. She took a step toward him but halted when Quinn cleared his throat behind her. She tried not to stare at Rayne's empty eye socket. He'd lost the eye in a fight during his last stint in prison for aggravated assault, and for some reason refused to wear an eye patch. He smiled at her, showing off the gaps in his mouth where he was missing teeth. "We just wanted to let you know this isn't over, Rayne. You know as well as we do you killed and dismembered those two women, and it's only a matter of time before you do something to screw up."

"You have nothing to link me to those murders. The last I heard, your DNA tests came back inconclusive." Rayne gave a shrug of his bony shoulders. His nose was crooked from one too many beatings, and the three-inch scar on his left cheek made an ugly man even uglier. His eyes were too close together and his long greasy hair—along with *everything* else about him—repulsed her. He'd no doubt repulsed those prostitutes too, which was most likely the reason he'd killed them so viciously. "I suggest you leave my establishment before I call my attorney and have charges pressed against you for harassment."

"You're a worthless little prick." Kay reflexively reached for her gun when he started toward her. Apparently, her words had struck a nerve with him. The revolver was pointing at his head before anyone had an opportunity to react. *Just give me a reason to blow your fucking brains out.*

"You have no right to talk to me like that!" Rayne's face was bright red with anger, and he ignored Quinn's orders to stand down. He took another step so he was within touching range of Kay. "Take it back."

Kay laughed. This was priceless. He was talking to her as if they were two little kids on the playground and she'd said something he didn't like. Did the idiot not realize she had a loaded gun pointed at his head?

"I won't take it back. In fact, I'll say it again. You're a worthless little prick, Tommy."

"You fucking cunt," he said menacingly. Quinn started to move between them, but it was too late. Rayne wasn't going to stop his tirade, and Kay had progressed beyond reason. "You ain't nothing but a skank whore bitch."

"At least I don't have to pay for sex, Tommy. When's the last time you got laid without having to pay for it? Was it in prison?"

"You fucking dyke!" He was reaching for her and she took a step back, the gun still aimed right between his eyes.

Kay didn't even think beyond the fleeting notion she'd be in one hell of a lot of trouble if she were to pull the trigger. Instead, she flipped the gun quickly so she was holding the barrel, and used all her strength to bring the butt of the gun across his face. The sickening sound of bones breaking was drowned out by Rayne's howl of anguish as he dropped at her feet.

Quinn took her gun without a word and set it on the counter before pulling out his cell phone and calling the lieutenant. Kay stood silently looking down at Rayne, who was crying and bleeding all over the floor in front of her.

There was no way this was going to turn out well. Kay was sure of it.

CHAPTER THREE

One month later

Kay sat alone at her kitchen table slowly sipping her third cup of coffee as she began week three of her eight-week suspension. She ran her fingers through her hair and leaned back in her chair. The black mark on her record was going to suck, but having to see the department shrink twice a week during the suspension was what really pissed her off. The suspension hadn't honestly surprised her. She remembered the exact second she'd crossed the line and knew she'd passed the point of no return.

It was when she'd gotten such a rise out of him when she called him a worthless little prick. She chuckled at the memory. Obviously, someone had used the term for him before. A past girlfriend? His mother? Or maybe it'd been one of the prostitutes he'd killed and cut to pieces. Her mind flashed back to the two women they'd found.

The first one had been a month earlier, found in a Dumpster behind the grocery store not a mile from Rayne's pawnshop. At least *most* of her had been found there. Her head and hands were left in another Dumpster a mile from his shop in the opposite direction. The woman's feet had never been found, and her heart had been crudely cut out of her chest. They hadn't been able to gather any DNA from the body because it had been thoroughly washed in bleach. The only thing they'd found on the body was a fiber from what they assumed was a washcloth, but even it was dismissed because of all the trash she was found in. They couldn't prove the fiber hadn't come from where she was dumped.

It was much the same with the second victim, only she'd been spread around to three different dump sites. Her remains were recovered a week after the first one, and again, they never found her feet, and her heart was gone. They couldn't officially call their suspect a serial killer until a third body was found, but they all knew what they were dealing with.

Questioning prostitutes wasn't her preferred assignment, but she'd gathered enough information to conclude the last person either of their victims was seen with was Tommy Rayne. He was well known among the hookers because most of them had turned down his business in the past. A lot of them also frequented his pawnshop if they needed some quick cash and their pimps weren't giving them enough to live on.

It rankled Kay to think Rayne was smart enough to kill these women and leave no trace of himself anywhere. They couldn't find the kill sites either. But what bothered Kay the most was the fact Rayne was able to get a restraining order against her. Her temper was well known around the squad room, but she'd always managed to keep her cool around suspects. Something about Rayne rubbed her the wrong way though. Other suspects had tried, and tried hard, to get under her skin before, but she'd never let them. Rayne seemed to know how to burrow his way in there and he refused to let go. Like a leech.

"You're letting it get to you, aren't you?" came a voice from behind her.

"Wouldn't you?" Kay asked with a sigh. She turned in her seat to look at her best friend, Fran Hodges. Fran's husband, Michael, was out of town on business, and Fran had spent the previous night in Kay's spare bedroom. "I'd like nothing more than to put a bullet in the man's head. I know he fucking killed those women, but he washes the bodies and leaves nothing behind. I'm convinced he's not that bright, Fran. How the hell is he getting away with this?"

"You need to relax, Kay," Fran said as she took the cup of coffee from her and poured it down the sink. "Can I make you some calming tea?"

Kay shook her head and watched as Fran poured a cup of coffee for herself. She'd do anything for Fran, which was why she didn't mind the sometimes-roommate when Michael was out of town on business. Fran hated staying alone at her own house. She was much more comfortable with Kay and Kay's three-year-old Rottweiler, Max.

Kay had gotten up at six, showered, and had intended to spend a little time in the hot tub before the contractor arrived to replace the deck and put up the privacy fence around her backyard. But then Rayne had managed to invade her thoughts again, and she'd spent the past hour sitting at the kitchen table drinking coffee.

She still wasn't entirely sure where the physical violence had come from. Kay had never been violent in her life—angry, yes, but not violent. God knew no one would have blamed her if she had been violent, considering the parents she'd been burdened with. They'd stifled her incredibly, and they'd never allowed her to truly enjoy her childhood.

Unlike her younger brother, Randall, who had always been the perfect little son. *He'd* been allowed to do anything he wanted to do and was never questioned about anything. It hadn't helped matters for Kay when he grew up and announced his intention to become a Catholic priest. Kay had never heard the end of it. They'd both been sent to Catholic school, and Kay often wondered if her parents had expected her to become a nun.

"Yeah, like that would ever happen," Kay said under her breath.

"What did you say?" Fran asked, taking a seat at the table with her.

"Just talking to myself."

"Uh-oh, that's never a good sign." Fran smiled and shook her head. "Means you're going crazy."

"Going? I'm already there. The trick is hiding the fact from the shrink." Kay went to the sliding glass door where Max was waiting patiently, his butt wagging since he didn't have a tail. He trotted in and went right to his food bowl. "I figure as long as I can resist answering myself, I'll be okay."

"You'll be okay regardless, sweetie. I'm going to grab a quick shower before I have to head out to work. I wish I could call out and stay here with you so I could see the hunky man who's going to build your fence."

"Trust me, he's no hunk if it's the guy who was here to give me the estimate." Kay laughed. Fran exited the room and Kay went to pour herself another cup of coffee. She loved Fran, but nobody stood between her and her morning joe. When she sat again, Max sat next to her, his head resting on her thigh, his big brown eyes looking up at her. She smiled and began to rub behind his ear with one hand.

She refused to allow Rayne any more of her energy, but the only other thing her brain could conjure was her family. She hadn't spoken to either of her parents in ten years. They'd disowned her when she'd come out to them. Even though she'd known their stance on homosexuality, she had never expected to be completely cut off from everything she'd ever known.

She honestly didn't know where she'd have ended up if it hadn't been for her uncle Norm. Kay's father's younger brother had been more of a father figure to her than he had been. Norm never married and had no kids, so when he died two years earlier, he'd left everything to Kay. Including a rather substantial amount of cash and investments.

The reading of Uncle Norm's will had infuriated her father, but Kay had gotten an obscene amount of joy out of it.

Even before her decision to become a police officer and her subsequent coming out fiasco, her father always enjoyed telling her she'd never be able to make it on her own—without a man—

and she took great pride in the fact she could now shove those words down his throat. Never mind the only reason she had this beautiful house in the first place was because of Uncle Norm. Kay was doing just fine on her own and wouldn't hesitate to point it out to her parents—if she were still talking to them.

With the intent of getting her mind off family, she decided to call Quinn and see how the investigation was going. Max sauntered into the living room when she grabbed the cordless phone from where it was charging by the sliding glass door leading out to the deck. She leaned her hip on the counter while the call went through.

"Quinn," he said gruffly, and Kay smiled. He was no doubt sitting behind his desk playing the same computer games he told her she shouldn't waste her time on.

"Hey, buddy, what's shakin'?" she asked.

"Griff, thank God. Tell me someone realized the error of their ways and you're coming back to this hell-hole earlier than expected. I need another adult I can talk to."

"Sorry, but no. I just called to see how you're doing."

"You mean you're calling to see if we've found anything on the worthless little prick," he said with a laugh. "There's nothing, Griff. He's covering his tracks. There's nothing at his pawnshop, nothing at his house. We've even gone to his ex-wife's house, and trust me, there's no love lost there. If she knew something that could help us, I have no doubt she'd tell us in a heartbeat. I can't figure out where he's killing these women."

"He'll screw up sooner or later. I just hope it's sooner so Paul and the brass don't pull the plug on us investigating Rayne."

"I hear ya," Quinn said quietly. "Webber has twenty-four hour surveillance on Rayne, but who knows how long it might last? He isn't going to do anything stupid while he has a tail."

"Unless he gets frustrated and loses his cool. We've seen it before."

"Yeah, keep your fingers crossed."

"Keep me updated."

"I will. Please hurry back here. These other idiots who call themselves homicide detectives can't carry on an adult conversation."

"Good-bye, Quinn."

Kay sighed and pulled her robe tighter around her body. She should probably change into something else since it was obvious she wasn't going to be getting in any time with the hot tub. The contractor was going to be there any minute.

CHAPTER FOUR

Brenda Jansen drove her rust bucket of a truck into the upscale neighborhood and looked around warily. Most people living in neighborhoods like this were suspicious of someone driving a beat up pickup truck like hers. The muffler needed to be replaced, and the back window had been smashed out—the result of having locked her keys inside the cab one day. Ever since then, she'd taken to carrying a spare key in her back pocket. It didn't matter though, what with the window being gone anyway.

It wasn't as though she couldn't afford a new truck. Hell, they had enough money in the bank to buy a whole new fleet of trucks for everyone who worked for her and her father. And she did have a brand new Durango she drove outside of work.

The simple fact was she had no desire to get rid of the old ugly truck. It'd been the first vehicle she'd ever bought with her own money. Yes, it was in rough shape, but it'd always gotten her through the workday. And it was hers. And she'd had it for fifteen years now. Maybe someday when it stopped being reliable she'd think about getting rid of it. There was a lot of sentimental value tied up in this truck.

Brenda glanced at the work order that was attached to her clipboard to double-check the address she was looking for. She hung her left arm out the window as she strained to see the addresses on the houses. When she finally spotted the one she was looking for, she pulled the truck into the double driveway, parking it right beside what looked to be a brand new Porsche.

After grabbing her clipboard, she opened the door and stepped out, immediately self-conscious about her appearance. She'd only taken this job today because Bill had called out sick. If she'd realized what neighborhood the job site was in, she would have given it to one of the other guys. When she'd gotten up that morning, she'd planned on working in the warehouse all day.

Her blue jeans were ripped along one outer thigh, and the other knee was worn to nothing but threads. Today, she'd decided to wear a white tank top that was maybe just a little too tight in the chest, and she was quickly beginning to regret her choice in attire. She went to the bed of the truck to get her toolbox, but then thought maybe she should go introduce herself to the homeowner first. It was a lot easier trekking through a stranger's house for the first time without lugging around the heavy box.

She definitely should have dressed more professionally, she thought as she looked at the car she was parked next to. If this job hadn't been forty-five minutes from the office, she would have seriously considered turning around and having someone else do it.

As she lifted her hair off her neck, she cursed under her breath at how unbelievably hot it was for nine o'clock in the morning. Brenda had always hated the summers in Pennsylvania, but she'd never lived anywhere else, so had no frame of reference for what pleasant summer weather might be. Carrying her clipboard in her right hand, she went up the walkway toward the front door and took a deep breath before ringing the bell. While she waited for someone to answer, she tucked the clipboard under her arm, pulled a rubber band out of her pocket, and quickly put her hair in a short ponytail.

"Hello, Mrs…" She glanced down at her work order again, and then back at the blonde who opened the door, trying hard to ignore the fact that the woman was wearing a bathrobe she'd neglected to tie at the waist. Based on the bikini she had on underneath, she looked as though she was planning on going swimming. "...Griffith. I'm from Jansen Construction. I'm here to replace your back deck and erect the fence around your backyard."

"It's Ms." The woman smiled as she looked Brenda up and down. Brenda tried her best not to stare at the woman's chest, but was having difficulty averting her eyes. When she did manage, though, her gaze was drawn to the tattoo of Tigger on her abdomen, right above her bikini line. Brenda cleared her throat nervously, wishing the woman would close the robe. "But please call me Kay."

"My name is Brenda, Ms. Grif...um, Kay." She somehow managed to force herself to concentrate on the green eyes openly appraising her. Something in her head told her she'd seen this woman before, but she tried to dismiss the thought.

"I was expecting a man," Kay said. Brenda could have sworn the woman was looking at her as if she knew her too. She would have been worried that Kay had donned her bikini to impress Bill if she hadn't been looking at Brenda with lust in her eyes. And if Bill hadn't been fifty pounds overweight and damn close to retiring age. "I expected the gentleman who was here before and gave me the estimate."

"Most people do expect a man in this business." Brenda couldn't suppress the smile tugging at the corners of her mouth. "Is the fact I'm a woman a problem for you? I can assure you the job will get done for the amount he quoted you. And just between you and me, I'll probably have it done in less time than it would have taken Bill. Of course, you'll be refunded for part of the labor if that's the case."

"What a shame it won't take longer." Kay smiled in a way Brenda could only describe as seductive, and then stepped aside to allow Brenda room to enter the house. "But of course it's not a problem."

Brenda waited a bit nervously while the door was closed behind her, and then she followed Kay into the kitchen. *Jesus, this woman is coming on to me.* Brenda smiled to herself at the thought. She'd heard some of the guys talk about things like this—women coming on to them when they showed up to do a job—but she'd never experienced it on a jobsite herself, and had never truly believed the guys' stories. And Kay didn't strike her as the lonely housewife type. Kay led Brenda to a sliding glass door in the kitchen and began to open it but stopped when a huge Rottweiler came and stood on the other side of the glass.

"You aren't afraid of dogs, are you?" Kay asked, finally pulling her robe closed and tying it at the waist. "He's a pussycat. Unless you're breaking in. Then he'll rip your throat out."

Brenda took a step back as she met her eyes. She loved dogs, but the visual Kay managed to put in her head with her words was a little alarming.

"No, he's fine," Brenda managed just before the door slid open and the dog jumped on her. She managed to stay on her feet, his front paws around her waist. His body wiggled furiously as she scratched behind his ears. "You're a big boy, aren't you?"

"Max, get down!" Kay shut the door again and took a stance that indicated superiority.

The dog obviously knew Kay was the alpha in the house and did as she commanded. He sat in front of Brenda with his head hanging down. His butt, however, continued its movement, albeit intermittently.

"We're still working on his rambunctious tendencies," Kay said with an affectionate smile as she looked at the dog. "I got him from a shelter a few months ago and his previous owners apparently had no boundaries for him. He's a good dog, though."

"Kay, sweetie, I'm leaving for work," said a woman who entered the kitchen, her hair still wet from a shower. The woman smiled at Brenda before placing a kiss on Kay's cheek. "Are you going to introduce me?"

"Fran, this is Ms…" She hesitated and then looked to Brenda for help. "I'm sorry. I don't believe you told me your last name."

"Jansen," Brenda replied as she held her hand out to Fran. "My name is Brenda Jansen."

"This is Fran." Kay finished the introductions, but her gaze never left Brenda's face, a flash of recognition in her eyes. Whether it was because Kay was surprised to learn her last name was the same as the company's name or if they'd met before, Brenda wasn't sure.

"I'm Kay's best friend." Fran smiled at Brenda and shook her hand briefly before squeezing Kay's hand and giving her a wink she obviously thought Brenda didn't see. "Call me later."

Best friend? Who were they kidding? It certainly looked to Brenda as though they were together. Or maybe it was just wishful thinking. Janice had always said Brenda assumed every woman was a lesbian. But really, who could blame her for hoping a woman as attractive as Kay Griffith might be gay?

"You two seem like a nice couple," Brenda said only because she wasn't quite sure what else to say in the awkward silence that followed Fran's departure.

"Couple?" Kay chuckled and shook her head. "Fran really is nothing more than my best friend. In fact, I've known her husband longer than I've known her. We grew up together."

Brenda smiled but said nothing as Kay led her out into the backyard. What was she supposed to think when Fran obviously had taken a shower in Kay's house at nine in the morning and then left to go to work? Brenda shoved the thoughts out of her mind. It wasn't any of her business.

"This job should only take about three or four days to complete," Brenda finally said after assessing the size of the yard and taking note of the materials Kay had purchased for the job. She turned back to face her and was pretty sure Kay had been checking her out. She decided to ignore it—at least for the moment. "I know Bill said it would take at least a week, but I don't think it should take that long. What will take the most time is tearing down the chain link fence and taking the deck apart. Installing the new materials will be a breeze, especially since you've been kind enough to supply it all for me."

"I figured it was the best way to make sure I got what I wanted." Kay was looking at her when Brenda turned to face her. "I'm sorry I keep staring at you, but I could swear I've seen you somewhere before."

Brenda shrugged and shook her head. It was beginning to bother her that Kay looked so familiar, and it was obviously disturbing Kay as well.

"Do you have a boyfriend, Ms. Jansen?"

"No, I don't." Brenda wasn't successful in stopping a short bark of laughter. "And please, call me Brenda."

"Why was my question so funny, Brenda?" Kay was smiling.

"I'm sorry." Brenda shook her head and regained her composure. She'd never even tried to hide the fact she was gay. "It wasn't funny at all. I'm not married. I don't have a boyfriend. Hell, I'm not even dating anyone at the moment."

Crap. Why the hell did I just tell her that?

"That surprises me. Are you happy being by yourself?"

Kay was definitely not shy, that much was sure. Usually, Brenda tried not to get too chummy with the clients. She *never* got to a first name basis with them, and she wondered briefly why Kay was different.

"It does get lonely sometimes," Brenda admitted. She noticed Kay's eyes were wandering again. She found herself once again regretting the decision to wear the tight tank top. Or maybe it hadn't been such a bad choice after all. She tried not to smile at the thought. "On the other hand, it's nice to not have to answer to anyone."

Kay met her eyes finally, and, no doubt knowing she'd been caught red-handed checking Brenda out, she had the decency to blush slightly.

"Okay, well then, I guess I'll let you get to your work." Kay headed back to the deck as she slipped the robe off her shoulders.

"I'll just be over here in the hot tub for a little while. I guess this will be my last chance for a few days. At least until you get the new deck put in."

Brenda followed her back to the deck, trying her damnedest not to stare at the perfect body revealed when the robe hit the ground. She continued through the house and out the front door to her truck, where she took a moment to catch her breath. She shook her head and thought about the blatant way Kay was flirting with her. *I've been out of the game for way too long. I don't even remember how to flirt back, for God's sake.*

After hefting the heavy toolbox from the bed of the truck, she began to walk back up the path to the front door, but stopped when she heard her cell phone ringing.

"Hello."

"Bren, it's me, Janice," came the voice from the other end. Brenda set the toolbox down and took a deep breath.

"What's up?" Brenda tried her best to sound as if she wasn't bothered by the call, when in reality it bothered her immensely. "I'm about to start a job, so I can't talk long."

"I thought you were working in the office today." The irritation was clear, even through the phone line. "I told you I wanted to come by this afternoon and pick up the rest of my things."

"I'm sorry my work schedule doesn't mesh with your plans, but maybe you should have thought about the difficulties in logistics *before* you cheated on me." Brenda took another deep breath while she listened to Janice muttering under her breath on the other end. "I can't just drop everything because you decide you need to get your things. I told you when you left it wasn't going to be easy scheduling a time to do this. Why didn't you just take it with you then? I mean, my God, if you haven't needed any of those things in the past year, what the hell would you need with them now?"

There was nothing but silence on the other end, and Brenda sighed in exasperation. Janice had left a little over a year earlier, and Brenda had since moved to a smaller apartment. She could have kicked herself for ever agreeing to take the rest of Janice's things with her in the first place. At the time, Brenda had gone through a short period when she'd hoped her lover of four years would change her mind and come home, but now, all she wanted was to be done with her.

"Fine," Brenda finally said. "I'll call you when I'm on my way home."

She hung up without another word, and just as she reached for the toolbox, the phone rang again. *Shit, shit, shit.*

"Not good enough for you?" she asked as she answered it again. The venom in her voice was undisguised, and she didn't care one bit. "I'm not about to rearrange my schedule."

"Whoa, Bren…let me guess," said Dana, her best friend since college. "You just got off the phone with The Bitch."

"I'm sorry, Dana." Brenda took a seat on the toolbox and closed her eyes. "She finally wants to come get the rest of her things. She's pissed at me because I'm ruining her plans."

"Oooh, I can just imagine *how* you're ruining her plans, and don't you dare tell me the real reason, because I'm sure my imagination can come up with something juicier." Brenda couldn't help but laugh at her. Dana always had a way of making her feel better, even when all hell was breaking loose around her.

"I can't talk right now. I have a job I'm supposed to be starting."

"All right, I just called to tell you I set up a date for you tonight with that woman I work with I told you about." Dana tried to keep talking, because she knew what Brenda's reaction would be to her statement.

"No," Brenda said adamantly. She pinched the bridge of her nose between her thumb and forefinger of her free hand. "You need to stop, Dana. I'll start dating when I'm good and ready to. Just apologize to her and tell her you made a mistake. Are we still playing at Discovery this weekend?"

"Unless you decide to back out of it too," was the aggravated response.

"Too? How the hell can I back out of a date I never agreed to in the first place? I'll talk to you later. I've got to get back to work now."

Brenda hung up and chuckled even though Janice had put her in a foul mood. She loved Dana, but the woman tried way too hard to fix her up. Why couldn't Dana just let her get back into the groove of things in her own time? She knew Dana meant well, but Brenda was beginning to get irritated with the whole thing.

Chapter Five

"Can I maybe interest you in a little lunch?" Kay asked when she walked out into the yard around one o'clock. Brenda glanced at her watch.

"I didn't realize it was this late." Brenda shook her head, and without thinking about what she was doing, she lifted the bottom of her tank top up to wipe the sweat from her forehead, exposing her torso. She quickly pulled the tank top back down where it was supposed to be and blushed slightly. "Sorry about that."

"Come inside, and I'll make you something to eat." Kay smiled slightly, and Brenda was relieved she chose not to comment on what she'd just seen.

Brenda hadn't allowed herself to notice earlier just how attractive Kay was. If she had, she never would have been able to look away when Kay entered the hot tub earlier. Thankfully, Kay had changed into a pair of shorts and a loose fitting T-shirt since then. She wore no makeup, but Brenda thought she didn't need it anyway.

"You don't have to feed me," Brenda said, kneeling to close the toolbox. "I can just run out and grab something."

"I want to," Kay answered.

Against her better judgment, Brenda followed and took a seat at the kitchen table where Kay indicated. As it turned out, Kay had already made sandwiches for them—ham and Swiss cheese. With mustard. Brenda *loved* mustard. She devoured hers a little too fast and then sat there, embarrassed, as Kay finished hers.

"I hope the sandwich was all right." Kay stood to clear the empty plates.

"It was great." Brenda nodded and tried to think back to the last time she'd eaten anything she hadn't gotten out of a can. Or the freezer. Unfortunately, she was drawing a complete blank. Her life had spiraled downward since Janice left her. Maybe she should have let Dana set her up with that woman. *Yeah, right.* "It's more than I would have eaten if I'd gone out to get something. I should probably be getting back to work though."

Not more than half an hour had passed when Brenda felt a hand on her shoulder. She turned to look, but the hand moved slowly across the top of her back, successfully sending a chill down her spine. Brenda closed her eyes and took in a deep breath. When she opened them again, Kay was standing by her side.

"Are you thirsty? I made some iced tea."

Brenda found herself wondering if this woman had a job. She must have one if she was able to afford a house in one of the most expensive housing developments in the area. Maybe it was just her day off. Brenda hoped she was right in her assessment, because Kay was becoming a distraction, and not just because she was making her lunch and afternoon tea.

"This isn't going to lower your price, you know." Brenda's joke went over the way she hoped it would. Kay's laughter was a full, rich sound that sent a shot of warmth through Brenda's belly.

They made their way to the deck and sat together at the table under a big umbrella. Brenda felt her pulse quicken when she looked at Kay, and now it was her turn to be embarrassed, as Kay caught Brenda checking *her* out.

"This is a really nice house." It was a lame thing to say, but Brenda was having problems forming her thoughts. Plus, she was more than a little uncomfortable at the silence surrounding them.

"Thanks." Kay smiled and glanced out at the yard. "I had a rich uncle who died and left me his fortune."

Brenda laughed, but she stopped abruptly when she saw by Kay's expression she was being totally serious.

"I'm so sorry. I thought you were kidding."

"I'm a cop. Trust me, I would never have been able to afford this house if it wasn't true. Norm never had kids, and I was his favorite niece, so…"

"You're a cop?" Brenda found herself intrigued in spite of herself. She allowed her mind to drift to Janice momentarily. "You work nights then?"

"No, believe it or not, I'm a homicide detective." Kay held her gaze as she spoke, and Brenda found it difficult to look away from her. "I'm out on suspension at the moment. I got just a little too rough with a suspect."

Brenda finally looked away and stared into her glass, not knowing what to say. Kay did not look like the stereotypical detective. Brenda had pegged her for an executive in an office high-rise downtown somewhere. Why she'd even tried to peg Kay as anything was a bit alarming to her. But now knowing that she was a cop, Brenda had another reason—besides the fact she was a client—to do something to squelch her attraction.

Janice worked in the forensics lab of Philadelphia's police department. She spent her days surrounded by cops. More than one seemed to have caught her attention, and she ended up having affairs with any woman she wanted. Once Brenda found out about it, Janice treated it like it wasn't a big deal. *Just sex,* was what she'd told Brenda. When Brenda reminded her cheating was the only thing she found intolerable in a partner, Janice left without so much as an apology.

"So what does Fran think about your suspension?" Brenda didn't really care, but was only trying to change the subject.

"You can go on thinking she's my girlfriend if you want, but she isn't. I'm single, just like you are." Kay ran a hand over

Max's head and he panted as he stared at Brenda. "She isn't my type anyway."

"What is your type?" Brenda was unable to stop herself from falling into Kay's trap. If she could have kicked herself, she would have.

"About your height, dark hair, brown eyes, good with her hands." Kay smiled when Brenda almost choked on her tea. The truth was Kay didn't have a type. Everything about a woman turned her on. But Brenda was turning her on simply because she was feigning disinterest. Usually women like this didn't warrant her attention, but Brenda was different. For some reason, Brenda's apathy was all about the game they were playing. "In other words, *you* are the epitome of what my type is."

"How convenient," Brenda said before swallowing what was left in her glass and standing. "I guess I walked right into that one, didn't I? I should be getting back to work though. Thank you for the tea."

Kay sat there in silence and watched Brenda walk back out to the fence. She'd never flirted so blatantly in her life and was thoroughly embarrassed, although she had to admit there was a part of her feeling tremendously exhilarated by it. The last thing she wanted to do was scare Brenda off. She'd be more than disappointed if Bill showed up the next day to work on her deck and fence.

Could she be reading the signs all wrong? What if Brenda wasn't gay? Just because she looked damned good in those jeans and the tight tank top—no, she'd never been wrong before. Her gaydar couldn't possibly be that far off, could it?

Kay managed to find things to keep herself busy so she didn't bother Brenda any further. She was sitting on the deck with a beer in her hand when Fran came home. Fran smiled at her as she took a seat across from Kay.

"She's cute, yes?" Fran asked, her eyes finding Brenda out in the yard.

"She thinks you're my girlfriend."

"I hope you explained the situation to her."

"I did, but it didn't matter. She thinks I'm lying." Kay set her beer down and glanced at Fran. "She's not just cute. She's fucking gorgeous, Fran."

"Maybe I need to put on my big-girl panties and spend the night at my own house then."

"No, you don't. I'm not in the practice of moving that quickly." Kay looked out in the yard and saw Brenda picking up her tools and putting things away for the day. She took a deep breath and tried not to think about the lump of disappointment in her gut. "I get the feeling she isn't as interested in me as I am in her anyway."

"Leaving so soon?" Fran asked Brenda when she made it up onto the deck. Kay resisted the urge to kick her under the table. "Why don't you join us for a drink?"

"Thanks, but I can't." Brenda smiled politely as she wiped some sweat from her neck.

"Sure you can. I know for a fact there's more beer in the fridge." Fran smiled innocently.

"Maybe some other time." Brenda looked at Kay. "I made sure to get the fence finished up tonight so you can let the dog out without a leash."

"Thank you. That was very thoughtful of you," Kay said, unable to take her eyes from Brenda's. "And Max thanks you too. Or at least he would if he wasn't zonked out somewhere else in the house."

"It's not a problem. I'll start on the deck first thing tomorrow morning, and I'll have someone come with me the following day so we can get everything finished up for you." Brenda nodded once in Fran's direction. "It was nice meeting you, and, Kay, thank you for lunch. I guess I'll see you in the morning. I can see myself out."

Kay nodded and smiled at her but didn't relax until she'd heard the front door close behind Brenda. When she looked back at Fran, she shook her head, knowing Fran's matchmaking tendencies.

"Off the charts good looks *and* she's polite. Your mother would be so proud."

"Yeah, except for the fact Brenda wasn't born with her genitalia on the outside. Which, I must say, is a deal breaker for dear old mom." Kay finished her beer and headed back into the kitchen, Fran right on her heels. "This kitchen needs a bit of modernizing, don't you think?"

"I was wondering what you were going to come up with to keep her around after the backyard is finished," Fran said with a laugh.

CHAPTER SIX

Brenda sat on her couch staring blankly at the television and drinking a diet soda that had ceased being cold at least an hour earlier. She wasn't paying attention to the show she had on and was a bit disconcerted to realize her thoughts kept returning to Kay Griffith.

Why wouldn't Kay just get out of her head? It had been so long since she'd had anyone flirt with her, she wasn't even sure how to respond. One thing she couldn't deny though—it felt incredibly good.

She'd called Janice when she was leaving Kay's house, but as usual, something else had come up, and Janice needed to schedule another time. The desire to throw her things in the Dumpster was growing more insistent by the day. So Brenda had stayed late at the office, hoping to clear her head with paperwork. She soon realized her feeble attempt to trick her own mind wasn't going to work, so she'd finally driven home to her one-bedroom apartment.

The place was rather sparse, with just the couch, coffee table, and a recliner in the living room. The television sat on top of an old TV cart on the far side of the room. In her bedroom, there was just the bed and a small dresser. She had a twenty-gallon fish tank in the living room as well, which her parents had given her. She kept the apartment clean, but it was incredibly lonely at times.

She'd made some disgusting frozen dinner that had tasted amazingly like cardboard and had promised herself—again—that she would start eating right. Soon. She used to cook for Janice all the time and was a pretty decent cook if she did say so herself. But since it was just her now, it seemed easier—albeit considerably less healthy—to eat the frozen and canned goods that didn't take much thought or preparation.

She leaned her head back on the couch and stared silently at the ceiling. No matter how hard she tried to think about other things, Kay's face—and body—managed to invade her mind. She couldn't stop thinking about the Tigger tattoo. Tigger, whose feet had been hidden below the bikini Kay had been wearing. She closed her eyes and cursed at herself under her breath.

"What the hell is wrong with you?" she muttered as she grabbed the remote and shut off the set. She was convinced she'd seen Kay somewhere before, and she hoped that was the reason Kay was still in her head. It was driving her nuts. Even though it was only nine o'clock, she decided she would just go to bed. As she stood, there was a knock on the door.

"I saw your light on." As usual, Dana didn't wait for an invitation; she walked past Brenda and straight to the bedroom door. "Why am I not surprised you're alone?"

"Why wouldn't I be?" Brenda shut the door and turned toward her.

"Exactly." Dana sat on the couch, but immediately stood again, a look of pain on her face as she rubbed her ass. "Shit! When are you going to get a new couch? That damned broken spring is going to kill somebody someday."

"You just need to know where to put your ass." Brenda smiled as she carefully resumed the same seat she'd occupied before. Dana opted to take the recliner instead, because it was much less dangerous. "And why would I need a new couch when this one is perfectly fine?"

"Whatever. So why didn't you want to go out tonight?" Dana leaned back in her chair. "She's a really nice woman. I think you two would hit it off."

"First of all, it's a Monday night, and I need to get up early tomorrow. Second, Janice was supposed to come by to get the rest of her things. Third, I hate blind dates. You know that, Dana. I hate them with a passion."

"I guess then I should be thankful you were alone. It's better than the alternative of having Miss Bitch in your bed again. You can't spend the rest of your life feeling sorry for yourself, Bren. Janice was an idiot, and she had no idea what she had. Don't let past experience turn you off of the possibility of another relationship."

"Don't forget about Nina," Brenda said. The mention of her previous lover caused Dana to laugh out loud.

"Please, Nina was nothing more than a gold digger. When she found out you wouldn't sign papers giving her your half of your father's business if something unfortunate were to happen to you, she jumped the first thing on two legs that had the misfortune to cross her path."

"I'm unlucky in love, Dana, and we both know it. It wasn't just the one experience of Janice cheating on me—with multiple women, let's not forget—but Nina cheated too." Brenda stared at the blank television screen and sighed. "You like to point out how I tend to latch on to women too quickly, remember? I want to just take time for me now. Maybe I need to get to know myself before I can figure out what I need from a partner."

"Don't go getting all philosophical on me, Bren."

"I'm just saying I think this past year has been good for me. Living alone with no pressure to please another person has given me a lot of time to think about the things I always do wrong when I meet a woman I like." Brenda shrugged and closed her eyes when Kay's image flashed in her mind again.

"When are you going to give me these fish?" Dana walked into the kitchen. Brenda could hear her searching the cupboards for junk food, but she came back empty-handed.

"You can have them any time you want to move the tank. I'm not helping though." Brenda shook her head. "I did not have fun moving it here after Janice left."

"I don't like seeing you alone, Bren. You're gorgeous, and you're in incredible shape. You're also almost forty years old. You need to move on, because you're sure as hell not getting any younger."

"I'm thirty-five, which is hardly *almost forty*." Brenda's tone was indignant, but it only made Dana laugh at her.

"You've met someone, haven't you?"

"How do you do that?" Brenda shook her head but avoided looking Dana in the eye.

"I've known you for fifteen years. I can tell when you're trying to hide something from me, and you should know by now it does absolutely no good. I always find out in the end."

"It's the woman I'm doing some work for right now." Brenda decided to just admit what she was thinking, because Dana was right. She did always find out in the end, so there was no reason to prolong the inevitable. Dana settled carefully next to Brenda on the couch.

"Tell me all about her." Brenda shook her head in amusement at the twinkle in Dana's eye and got comfortable as Dana put an arm through hers and leaned her head on Brenda's shoulder. "And don't you dare leave anything out."

"There's nothing to tell." *But there must be, or I would be able to stop thinking—no, fantasizing—about her.* "She's a cop. And I think she has a girlfriend, but she denies it."

"Bullshit. There's got to be more." Sometimes Brenda hated the fact Dana knew her so well. "If that was all, then you wouldn't be sitting here thinking about her."

"She was flirting with me." Brenda shrugged slightly. "She made me lunch too, and I could swear I've seen her somewhere before."

"She's a cop? Maybe you met her somewhere with The Bitch." Dana squeezed her arm and sat up to look at Brenda, her brow furrowed. "Or maybe she's someone The Bitch slept with."

It wasn't something Brenda even wanted to consider, but she couldn't deny the thought had crossed her mind. Kay did work in the Philly police department, but Brenda had no idea if she was working out of the same precinct where Janice's office was. She wasn't even going to mention her concerns to Dana though. Dana had a way of talking things to death—to the point where Brenda would end up so stressed out she wouldn't be able to think straight.

"You're going back there tomorrow, right?" Dana changed the subject, no doubt sensing Brenda's discomfort with the ideas she'd raised. "Flirt back." She waved a hand when Brenda opened her mouth to protest. "I'm telling you, if she flirts with you again, play along. No matter how far it goes, don't back down."

"She's with someone. I've been the one cheated on too many times to ever get involved with someone who's already got a partner."

"You said she denied the girlfriend thing, right?"

"You don't think people lie? You don't think Nina and Janice lied to all the women they slept with? Because they sure as hell lied to me about it."

"Find out if she's telling you the truth." Dana was insistent if nothing else. "Sometimes you just have to put your faith in someone, sweetie. And I want to hear all about it at rehearsal tomorrow night."

Brenda finally agreed reluctantly.

"Are you seeing anyone now?" Brenda didn't want to talk about Kay any more.

"Why? Are you finally realizing I'm the woman of your dreams?" Dana winked at her but didn't wait for an answer, because it was always the same response. "I've hooked up with Nancy."

"Our bass guitar player Nancy?" Brenda was a bit surprised. Nancy had to be at least ten years younger than Dana.

"She is an animal in bed." Dana smiled, and Brenda laughed. "An absolute *animal*, Bren. It's not going to last though. She's way too young for me, but it'll be fun for a while."

"I'm confused about something. The last four or five people you've been with have been women. What happened to the whole bisexual thing?"

"Oh, please, I am so over that." Dana laughed as she slapped Brenda playfully on the forearm. "I'm not getting any younger either. While it's been fun playing both sides of the fence, it's time for me to find the woman who can finally tie me down. Men just don't seem to do it for me anymore."

Dana stood before Brenda had a chance to respond and leaned over to kiss her on the cheek before letting herself out—gone again as quickly as she had breezed in. Brenda shook her head and chuckled to herself, but then Kay was there in her mind once again

Brenda closed her eyes, emotionally drained. She went to bed, and as she lay there wide-awake, she tried to concentrate on where she might have seen Kay before. She was pretty certain it didn't have anything to do with Janice because she couldn't place the two of them together anywhere. She finally sighed in frustration.

What if Kay was single? It was possible she could have been telling the truth about her relationship with Fran. Maybe she should flirt back as Dana suggested. God knew Kay was the first woman she'd been even mildly attracted to in the past year. And *mildly* didn't even begin to describe it. Kay was hot. *Smoking* hot.

Since Janice left, she'd gone to the bars a few times, but she always went home alone. She hadn't dated at all and knew Dana was right—she needed to get out there and meet people. The problem was, her heart just wasn't in it.

Her days consisted of work, more work, and sleep. Occasionally, their band would play a gig on the weekends. Lately though, she hadn't even been eating right. She kept herself in shape by working and going to the gym once in a while. She'd somehow managed to convince herself she didn't need a woman in her life to make her happy.

Brenda let out an exasperated sigh as she turned onto her side so she was now staring at the alarm clock instead of the ceiling. Unfortunately, the change in scenery hadn't altered her thinking patterns. If she wasn't dwelling on how Janice had hurt her, it was Kay Griffith. *Where the hell have I seen you before?*

"Damn it." Brenda turned onto her other side and closed her eyes tightly. "Just get the fuck out of my head."

The vision of Kay opening her front door wearing her bikini and showing off her tattoo was the last coherent thought Brenda had before finally drifting off to sleep.

Kay was lying in bed, but she was wide-awake. Brenda Jansen just would not get out of her mind, no matter how hard she tried. She made a concerted effort to think about work, but it was going to be several weeks before she would be allowed back. What good would it do to think about things she had no control over?

After about half an hour of trying unsuccessfully to capture sleep, she threw the sheet off her naked body and got up. She grabbed her robe from the foot of the bed and put it on as she headed downstairs to the kitchen. Max jumped off the bed and trotted happily behind her all the way through the house.

She pulled a beer from the fridge and went out to try to relax on the back deck. Jesus, even at almost eleven o'clock at night it was nearly too sweltering to be outside. The humidity was horrendous in Pennsylvania mid-August.

She sat back and stared out at the length of new fence Brenda had put up. It was six feet tall and made for privacy, so she could use the hot tub naked without fear of the neighbors seeing her. Kay had always wanted a hot tub, and it was the first thing she'd added after buying the house three months earlier. She smiled at Max, who was running along the fence sniffing every step of the way. He'd been doing the same thing every time she'd let him out since Brenda left earlier in the evening. She wasn't so sure Max liked the new fence, but Kay did.

Her phone rang and Kay considered letting the machine pick it up, but then decided against it. It might be Fran calling to say she reconsidered and wanted to sleep in the guest room again. She reached inside the door for the cordless phone.

"Hello."

"Hey, Griff, how are you holding up?" It was her lieutenant, Paul Webber. It had to be a personal call, because if it had been business, he would have called her on her cell. But then again, he wouldn't call her cell because she was out on suspension. "You're keeping your appointments with the shrink, right? I can't afford to have you out any longer than another few weeks."

"Yes, Paul." She couldn't help but smile. Paul was always looking out for her. "Everything is going according to schedule. Something tells me if it weren't, you'd know about it."

"You're probably right." He sounded tired.

"What's up?" Kay glanced at her watch and saw it was ten thirty. "You've never called this late just to chat."

"My wife asked about you tonight, and I started thinking about you. I hadn't talked to you in a while, and thought I should call and see how you're holding up."

"I'd feel a lot better if I knew you'd arrested Tommy Rayne for those murders."

"Kay, I can't discuss the case with you. You know that."

Kay sighed as she shook her head and resumed her seat on the deck. After a drink from her beer, she cleared her throat. Paul was right. He couldn't discuss the case with her. But it didn't mean she couldn't say something to him about it.

"Rayne was the last one seen with both of those women, Paul. He cut them up and dumped them in the trash."

"Kay, please."

"The dump sites were too close to his pawnshop for it to be a coincidence." Kay paused and heard nothing but soft breathing coming from the other end of the line. "You know as well as I do he's guilty."

"It doesn't matter what any of us think, Griff. The fact of the matter is, there's no evidence to say he's our guy. Don't worry about it, all right? We're watching him, and if he so much as jaywalks, he'll be hauled in."

Kay couldn't ask for much more, could she? Paul always looked out for her.

"If you ever need to talk, you know I'm here for you, right?"

"Thanks, Paul." Kay swiped at the tear threatening to roll down her cheek. She'd been in homicide for nine years, and Paul had taken her under his wing. He'd always been like a second father to her, next to Uncle Norm, of course. "You have no idea how much it means to me right now."

"You should get some sleep." Paul cleared his throat and became more businesslike. It was his usual defense mechanism whenever Kay turned serious on him. He was uncomfortable with anyone seeing his softer side. "We'll be waiting for you to get back to work."

She hung up and sat there for a moment in silence. She blew out the candle before standing and taking her beer inside to dump what was left of it. Once back in bed with Max curled up at her feet, she found herself staring at the ceiling again.

She thought about resigning from the force. It wasn't the first time it had crossed her mind, and she was sure it wouldn't be the last. The frustration level with how things were done weighed heavily on her. The disillusionment started three years earlier when a murderer was set free on a technicality. They'd done everything by the book, but the lab mishandled the evidence. Because of that, the man they all knew brutally killed an elderly couple in a robbery gone bad was set free. He murdered his mother and girlfriend two weeks later. The case made her rethink her priorities, and she constantly found herself wondering if she was doing any good at all.

And now there was this. She didn't feel any better about Rayne after her talk with Paul, but she was surprised he wasn't at the forefront of her mind. Brenda was still there invading her thoughts and taunting her with the possibility they'd met somewhere before. Where the hell could it have been?

Kay tried unsuccessfully to place Brenda's face in the grocery store, the dry cleaners, and even the gas station down the street, but she just didn't seem to fit in any of those places.

The police station? No. That wasn't it. She knew if she didn't stop this, it would no doubt succeed in driving her to the nuthouse.

When she finally drifted off to sleep, it was only to dream about Brenda Jansen in her sports bra, and they were in the hot tub together.

CHAPTER SEVEN

Brenda cursed as she slammed a fist down on the dashboard of her truck. She loved the truck, but even she had to admit it was a piece of shit. Why it hadn't refused to start *before* she left the office she didn't know. Of course it had decided to wait until she stopped at a convenience store to get herself a cup of coffee and a big bottle of water. She wondered who to call first—Kay or the office. Her father's voice echoed in her head.

Always put the customer first. It was a mantra he'd drilled into her over the years. After all, if the customer wasn't happy, then nobody was happy. Brenda grabbed her cell phone.

"Hello," Kay said

"Kay," Brenda said, her heart skipping a beat at the sound of Kay's voice. Brenda wondered briefly if she should have called her Ms. Griffith. Too late now. "This is Brenda Jansen. I'm running a bit late this morning. I'm afraid my truck won't start, and I'm about halfway to your house. I'm going to have to call the office and have someone bring my other vehicle to me. My best guess is I'm going to be about another hour or so."

"No, that's not acceptable." Kay's tone was firm.

"Pardon me?"

"I'm sorry, but I have an appointment I have to keep this morning. I can't wait that long for you to get here. I'll come pick you up then you can have someone bring your other vehicle to you at my house. Tell me where you are."

Brenda hesitated, wondering what the hell was happening. She told Kay, though she was shocked she had. Why in the world would she allow a customer to pick her up and give her a ride to the job site? There seemed to be something very unprofessional about it. Especially considering it would take Kay at least the same amount of time to come pick her up and drive back home as it would have for Brenda to wait for someone to bring her truck to the store.

After they hung up, she called the towing company to come and pick up the scrap heap. It was definitely time to junk it once and for all. Then she called Grace at the office, told her what had happened, and they made arrangements for someone to bring her Durango to her at Kay's house later in the morning.

She'd just finished unloading everything from her truck when Kay pulled into the parking lot next to her. Brenda assumed that the Porsche in her driveway the previous morning had belonged to Fran. Kay was driving a dark blue Explorer now.

Brenda placed a note on the windshield of the pickup for the tow truck driver.

"What is this?" Kay held up the case she was putting into the back of her SUV.

"My drums. I'm in a band, and we're rehearsing tonight."

"Very cool." Kay smiled and nodded in approval. "Where do you play?"

"We're playing at a club called Discovery this weekend." Brenda stole a look at Kay from the corner of her eye. She noticed Kay glance at her and then smile. "You've heard of it?"

"Yes, but I've never been inside. The club is next door to a pawnshop we had to go to in order to question a suspect in a murder investigation." Kay smiled and shrugged. "He was not very cooperative."

Everything fell into place for Brenda. Her expression must have spoken volumes about what was going through her mind, because Kay laughed out loud.

"You're the cop who broke Tommy Rayne's nose."

"You know him? Is he a friend of yours?"

"God, no." Brenda shook her head and a wave of disgust swept through her, causing a shiver to run down her spine. She wanted to shake Kay's hand for having had the balls—figuratively speaking, of course—to break the scumbag's nose. "He's an asshole. You know, it would be a nice neighborhood if it weren't for his shop. He's always got seedy looking people coming and going. I have no doubt he deserved what you did to him."

"Oh, he most definitely did." Kay smiled and nodded her head emphatically. "All in the course of a sentence or two, he managed to call me a skank, a whore, a bitch, and a dyke. Actually, I think it was *fucking* dyke. I lost it. My partner tried to hold me back, but I swear I'd never been so pissed off in my entire life. Now, you have to understand my partner is about six foot five, and is probably somewhere in the neighborhood of two fifty."

"Damn, you must be one hell of a tough woman." Kay was pretty much the same height as her at five foot nine, and she couldn't weigh more than one forty, soaking wet. "I read about it in the paper, but when you told me your name yesterday, it didn't click. That must be why you look so familiar to me."

"No, I think it just occurred to me where we've met. You were at Paul Webber's Fourth of July picnic last year, right? You were there with Janice Green."

"You know Janice?" Brenda turned her head and looked out the window so Kay couldn't see the anger in her eyes. If Janice slept with Kay…

"She's our forensics guru. How do you know her?"

"We were together for almost four years. That picnic was the last time I saw her. She left me for the flavor of the month."

"I'm sorry," Kay said, and Brenda thought she wanted to say something else, but Kay just shook her head and concentrated on driving.

They rode the rest of the way in silence, and Brenda kept catching herself looking over at Kay, wondering what she was thinking. She was also wondering why she was feeling this way when she was around Kay. It was almost as though there was an electric current between them. After Janice left, Brenda had just felt numb. She'd convinced herself she would never feel that level of desire again, but she was now, and it made no sense to her. Could all of this possibly be because Kay flirted with her the day before? If that was the case, then she certainly needed to get out more.

And she needed to find out if Kay had been one of Janice's many transgressions.

Brenda worked all morning without a break, mostly because she wanted to get this job done and get out of there. Maybe then she could stop fantasizing about Kay. She looked at her watch and saw it was noon, so she closed her toolbox and sat on top of it with a sigh.

The bottle of water she'd brought with her was on the ground next to her feet, and she picked it up, swallowing what was left of it in one drink. As she pulled her shirt out of her jeans to wipe the sweat and water from her face, she glanced up and saw Kay standing just inside the sliding glass door watching her.

She motioned for Brenda to come and join her. Brenda considered declining the offer, but she needed a break, so she replaced the top on the water bottle and walked into the house.

Kay had brought a pizza home with her after her appointment. Brenda saw there were paper plates and napkins out for them. They settled in at the kitchen table, Brenda with an iced tea, and Kay with a beer.

"You don't drink?" Kay asked her.

"Not while I'm working." Brenda shook her head. There was an awkward silence, so she tried to make polite conversation. "So, how long have you been a cop?"

"Forever," Kay said, rolling her eyes and laughing. "At least it seems like it to me. I got out of the academy when I was twenty-two, which was twelve years ago."

"There's no way you're thirty-four," Brenda said. She knew it sounded like a line as soon as the words left her mouth, but it was the truth. She would have guessed thirty, at the most.

"Thank you." Kay nodded and smiled. "But I am. I spent a little while as a beat cop, and for the past almost nine years I've been in homicide. It's pretty much a good old boy network, but for the most part, they're cool with me. Of course, there are a few exceptions to the rule."

Brenda struggled with the question she'd wanted to ask since they'd been in the car that morning, mostly because it was inappropriate to ask a customer personal questions. But she had to know for her own peace of mind.

"Did you ever…you know…you and Janice…" She couldn't do it. She met Kay's eyes and could tell Kay knew exactly what she was trying to ask.

"Did I sleep with her?" Kay asked after a moment. Brenda nodded. "No. I've never had anything more than a professional relationship with her. With anyone at work, honestly."

"Do you know anyone she has slept with?"

Kay shook her head, and a part of her wanted to strangle Janice. Brenda didn't seem like a woman to be cheated on. Kay couldn't imagine doing it. If Brenda were hers…no, she couldn't go there. Brenda had obviously been hurt and would no doubt have a difficult time trusting anyone.

"She's in a relationship right now. Just under a year."

"If you know the woman, you should warn her. She started cheating on me right before our first anniversary. Silly me, I believed her when she said it would never happen again. Right before the picnic last year, I had to run home because I'd forgotten something. I walked into the bedroom and there she was, her face buried between some woman's legs. I just stood there, not believing what I was seeing. I was numb. I guess when the other woman finally came, it snapped me out of it. I went to the bed and grabbed Janice by the hair and pulled her off."

Kay listened quietly, knowing somehow Brenda needed to get it all off her chest. It broke Kay's heart to hear how she'd been hurt, and the next time she saw Janice she'd tell her exactly what she thought of her.

"She screamed, but then when she saw me she started crying and told me how much she loved me. When I told her I didn't want to hear it, she turned vicious. Told me I was stupid if I thought this was the only time she'd cheated." Brenda paused and looked at Kay, but Kay had the feeling she wasn't seeing her at all. She had the look of someone caught up in a memory. "She told me there'd been at least ten others. I swear to God, I wanted to kill her in that moment. I probably would have if I'd had a gun."

Kay tried to ignore it when Brenda wiped away a tear, but she couldn't. She moved her chair so it was next to Brenda and put an arm around her shoulders. She was a little surprised when Brenda let her head rest on Kay's shoulder. Without thinking, Kay smoothed Brenda's hair and pulled her closer. It felt good to hold a woman in her arms.

"I'm sorry," Brenda said after a moment. She pulled away and got to her feet before looking around as though she didn't know where she was.

"You have nothing to be sorry for, Brenda," Kay assured her. She fought not to show how the loss of contact affected her. For a moment, she felt as though she were adrift at sea with nothing to anchor her down. She forced a smile she hoped was reassuring. "I'm a pretty good listener if you ever need to talk about something."

"I need to get back to work."

Kay watched, feeling more helpless than she ever had before as Brenda went back to ripping apart her deck. More than anything, Kay wanted to make everything better for Brenda, but knew she couldn't.

Besides, being the knight in shining armor wasn't really her thing. At least it never had been before now.

CHAPTER EIGHT

"Well, I'm all done for today," Brenda said at the end of the afternoon. She glanced at her watch and saw it was four o'clock. They still hadn't brought her truck to her, and she must have phoned the office twelve times throughout the day. "I called again, and they said someone would be here soon. I'm not sure what exactly that means since they were supposed to have it here this morning, but I'll just go and wait out front with my drums if you'd be so kind as to open the garage for me."

"Don't be silly," Kay said, shaking her head. "You're more than welcome to wait right here and have a drink with me."

She went into the kitchen and brought two beers out to the deck for them.

"Thanks." Brenda smiled uneasily and took the bottle, but wasn't completely sure she wanted it. She was still a little embarrassed about her meltdown earlier and just wanted to get the hell out of there.

"We could go in the hot tub since you left that part of the deck intact until tomorrow," Kay said, and Brenda raised one eyebrow.

"Damn, I completely forgot to bring my swimsuit with me today," Brenda said in response. Kay smiled and took a sip of her beer.

"Who said you needed one?"

Brenda couldn't help but chuckle as she looked away, hoping her nervousness wasn't apparent. She cleared her throat and then put her hands up and shrugged.

"I'm afraid I don't have a snappy comeback for that," she said.

They sat across the table from each other and their eyes met for a brief moment. Brenda wished she knew whether Kay was available or not. The pull she felt toward her was incredibly strong, but she knew she had to play it cool. Her usual way of jumping into a relationship too quickly needed to change. The way things ended with Nina and Janice both were proof of that.

"Listen, I was thinking about putting in a pool," Kay finally said. Her voice sounded a little shaky to Brenda. "Do you think you could do it for me?"

"You should call someone who specializes in pools," Brenda answered, shaking her head. "We don't even do fences like this usually. Mostly we do add-ons, remodels, and things like that. And with those floods we've had over the past few years, we've been pretty busy with all the remodels. Hopefully, we won't have any more floods. While it's good for business, it sure as hell wreaks havoc on people's lives."

"Oh," Kay said, the disappointment obvious in her tone and demeanor. "How about remodeling the kitchen? It could certainly stand to be a little more modern."

Brenda smiled and shook her head as she leaned forward.

"If you want me to come back here, Ms. Griffith, maybe you should just try asking," she said quietly. She was so out of practice with this flirting business. It was so much harder than she remembered it being.

"That would work?" Kay asked, eyeing her a bit suspiciously.

"I'm not sure," Brenda confided as she sat back again. "But you could try it, instead of just making things up for me to work on for you."

"Okay," Kay said slowly. She picked up her beer and took a drink. When she set it back down, she took a deep breath. "Would you like to come over for dinner tomorrow night?"

Brenda looked at her, and she felt the smile on her face begin to fade. Her heart was racing. Had she really expected Kay to ask? To call her bluff? What was it Dana had said to her? *Flirt back. No matter how far it goes.*

Brenda hadn't expected a dinner invitation. She cleared her throat, but when she spoke it still sounded to her as if her throat was a bit constricted. Her voice wanted to break, but she somehow managed to keep it under control.

"What are you doing?" she asked quietly as she shook her head.

"I don't understand." Kay looked confused.

"You don't even know me, Kay."

"But that's the point, isn't it? People date in order to get to know each other. At least I think that's how it goes. It's been a while for me."

"You're asking me on a date?"

"Yes, I guess I am."

"I went home last night and I couldn't stop thinking about you," Brenda said, and was shocked as the words came out of her mouth. Why in God's name was she telling her this?

"I had the same problem."

"I don't think I can do this," Brenda said. "I don't talk to anyone about Janice, and I've only known you for two days. You got me to open up about her, and I even fucking cried in front of you. I can't do this."

"Can't do what? What is it exactly you're doing?"

"There hasn't been anyone since her. I can't do casual sex anymore. I got it all out of my system before I met her. And I'm too damned old to start all over again."

"So you're just going to be alone for the rest of your life?"

"It's a hell of a lot simpler." Brenda nodded. God, why couldn't her heart just follow her head for once? Why did it have to have a mind of its own that seemed to control everything below her waist?

"All I want is to get to know you a little better. A date doesn't mean we have to end up in bed, you know. We share a meal, and who knows? We might find out we can't stand each other. Problem solved."

"I can't do this," she said again as she stood. The problem was Brenda *did* want to do this, no matter what her head was telling her. Her heart was winning this battle, and she knew she had to get out of there before it was too late. Before she did something she would regret. The job was almost done, and she could walk out of there without ever having to see Kay again.

Kay followed her to open the garage door so she could get her drums out. Brenda steadfastly refused to even glance her way as she moved her equipment onto the driveway. She sat on her toolbox and stared down the road. After a few seconds, Kay came and stood in front of her, blocking her view. Brenda shielded her eyes from the sun and looked up into her face.

"You're coming back tomorrow, right? I can't have my back deck unfinished."

Brenda felt her heart speed up at the sight of Kay standing above her, hands on her hips. She had the feeling Kay didn't know just how sexy she was.

"I'll be here with help so we can finish it all up tomorrow. I'll be out of your hair by this time tomorrow."

Brenda squinted, trying not to let on how much the sunlight was bothering her. Kay stood there looking down at her. After a moment, she nodded once and walked away.

"That would be a good thing if I actually wanted you out of my hair."

Once Kay was safely back inside the house, Brenda was finally able to take a deep breath. She wasn't about to admit it to her, but there was something about Kay that was chipping away at her defenses. The problem was, she wasn't sure she was at all happy about it.

She glanced up when she heard an engine rev, hoping it was someone from the office with her Durango. Instead, she saw a sixty-five Mustang that had seen better days. It looked as though the owner hadn't put any money into it other than to tint the windows so no one could see inside. The driver stopped at the end of Kay's driveway and revved the engine again before taking off, tires squealing loudly just before she heard the thump of the bass as it turned around the corner and was out of sight.

Brenda wondered if she should tell Kay about it but ultimately decided there was no point. And besides, Hank, their warehouse manager, was just pulling into the driveway with her Durango. She glanced back at the house and saw Kay watching through the front window before she began loading her things into the back of the truck.

CHAPTER NINE

B renda walked into the bar a bit late for rehearsal that evening, thanks to Hank not having someone follow him in another vehicle so she had to take him back to the shop first. Dana made her way over to Brenda immediately. Brenda shook her head and held up a hand as she went to work setting up her drums. Dana never could take a hint though and kept badgering her. Brenda finally grabbed her by the arm and pulled her away from the other two band members.

"I don't want to talk about this right now," she said firmly. "I had a colossally shitty day that started when my damn truck crapped out on me, and ended with me getting here almost a half hour late. So let's please get this damn rehearsal over with so I can just go home and crash."

Dana threw up her hands and walked away, and Brenda went to the bar to get a soda. By the time they finished rehearsal two hours later, Brenda felt a little better, because she'd been able to take out some of her frustrations by banging on the drums.

She knew she was going to have to tell Dana about her day, because Brenda was the one who always gave her a ride home after they were done rehearsing. She found herself hoping since Dana had hooked up with their guitar player, Nancy, that maybe she would take her home.

No such luck. At least they practiced in the city tonight. When Carol, the owner of Discovery, had other things planned for the bar, they rehearsed at Nancy's house in Camden. Brenda preferred rehearsing in the city not only because it was a lot less hassle to get home, but the acoustics were better in the bar than in Nancy's basement.

"Your little affair with Nancy over already?" Brenda asked as they stood outside so Dana could smoke a cigarette. Brenda didn't smoke and never allowed anyone to smoke in the Durango.

"No, I just wanted to be alone tonight," Dana said with an indifferent shrug. "And I wanted to hear about what happened with this mystery woman today, since you weren't very forthcoming about it earlier."

Brenda looked at her watch impatiently and glanced up the street to see Tommy Rayne coming out of his pawnshop, locking it up for the night. She took Dana's arm and started to push her in the other direction.

"You dykes are a little early," he called out. "They don't usually open until ten."

"You don't even sound like your nose is broken, Tommy," Brenda called back to him as she let go of Dana's arm and turned back toward him. She knew she shouldn't antagonize him, especially when he was a suspect in a murder case, but she couldn't help herself. He was the biggest ass she had ever met in her life.

"What the hell do you know about it?" he said, but he stayed where he was, which was only about fifteen feet away. Obviously, he wasn't quite ready to challenge anyone yet. Not even two women with no traffic in sight.

"I know it was a woman who beat the crap out of you," she said. Dana grabbed her arm and tried to get her to shut up. Brenda turned to her. "What? It was in the papers. It's common knowledge."

"Just don't push his buttons. He scares the crap out of me," she said as she threw her not quite finished cigarette on the ground and stamped it out with the heel of her boot. She put her arm through Brenda's and pulled her in the opposite direction, toward the Durango. After they'd gotten inside and locked the doors, Dana turned to look at her. "What the hell is wrong with you?"

"It was her," Brenda said, and in spite of her foul mood, she found herself smiling. "The woman I was doing work for? She's the one who broke his nose."

"No fuckin' way," Dana said, and then she laughed. "She's the cop that went berserk and got suspended?"

Brenda nodded as she pulled out into the street and headed down the road.

"So what else did you find out about her today?" Dana asked a few minutes later.

"She was trying to think up other jobs for me to do when I'm finished there tomorrow."

"I think you should go for it," she said. "It could be fun. What have you got to lose?"

"She knows Janice. She says she never slept with her, but how do I know she's telling the truth?"

"Not everybody is a liar, Bren. Just because she knows her doesn't mean anything happened between them. Shit, I know The Bitch, and you can be damn sure I never slept with her."

"I know you're right," Brenda finally conceded.

"So what's the problem then? She's interested, and I know you are, so seriously, what's the problem? Just go with it. You're both adults."

"She invited me to dinner at her house tomorrow night." Brenda pulled into Dana's apartment complex and found an open space next to her front door.

"I suppose it's safe to assume you turned her down?"

"Yes, I did."

"I think you're making a big mistake, but it's your life." Dana reached for the door handle, but then stopped and turned back to Brenda. "Look, it's only nine o'clock. Call her. Or even better, go to her house. Apologize for whatever it was you said to her, because knowing you, you did say something wrong, and just see where it gets you."

"Good night, Dana," she said, giving her a half-hearted shove on the arm. "Get the hell out of my truck, and I'll see you Friday night."

As she pulled out of the lot, Brenda turned the opposite direction she should have gone in order to get home. It wasn't something she'd done on purpose, and in fact, her mind was so busy going over the conversation she'd had with Kay earlier, she didn't even notice where she was headed. As it turned out, she ended up only a few minutes from Kay's house.

She pulled into a grocery store parking lot and decided to pick up some soda and maybe some junk food or something else to munch on.

"Brenda?" a voice from behind her called.

As she locked the doors to her SUV, she turned to see who it was, dreading—and hoping at the same time—it would be Kay. It wasn't though. *Damn.*

"I'm sorry. Did I get your name right?" the woman asked hesitantly. "I'm Fran, Kay's friend. We met at her house yesterday."

"Yes," she answered with a nod as Fran walked toward her.

"Do you live around here?" Fran asked. They walked the rest of the way to the store entrance side by side.

"No, I was just dropping off a friend and decided to stop here for a few things," Brenda replied, trying her best to smile politely.

"Listen, I was on my way to Kay's, just for a beer," she said, and then she smiled as though she'd just solved all the world's problems. "Why don't you come along?"

"It's a little late, isn't it?" Brenda asked, looking at her watch. It was a quarter past nine. Maybe it wasn't too late. What was late for one person may not be for another.

"Well, I don't work tomorrow, and I guess she told you she's been suspended, so it doesn't matter to us what time it is," she explained. She put a hand on Brenda's arm. "I know she would love to see you."

"I don't think so," Brenda said, shaking her head. She realized she'd love to see Kay too. "I need to get up early tomorrow."

"What would it hurt to have one beer with us?" Fran asked. Brenda just shrugged indifferently, and when she didn't say anything, Fran apparently decided to spill Kay's secrets. "She likes you, Brenda. She must have called me twenty times over the past two days, just to talk about you. She's worried she won't ever see you again."

"Why should it matter to her?" Brenda asked with a shake of her head. She stepped out of the way as a couple walked past them into the store. When they were gone, she looked at Fran again. "She doesn't even know me."

"I know things can't be that much different in our worlds," Fran said with an exaggerated sigh. "You've never hooked up with someone you just met in a bar? I'd be willing to bet you know more about each other than you would in that situation."

"I don't do casual, which *is* something she knows about me," Brenda said. She tried to step around Fran, but Fran moved to block her path. Brenda met her eyes defiantly and refused to look away. "I need to go."

"Are you really so thickheaded you can't see how she looks at you?"

"She just met me yesterday," Brenda pointed out what should have made perfect sense, except she couldn't lie to herself. There was something about Kay that intrigued her. "She could go into a bar and have any woman she wants."

"But she wants you. I'm not going to beg, and I'm sure Kay is going to be pissed at me for talking to you about this anyway. I just don't see what the harm would be for you to come and have a beer with us."

Brenda stared at her in silence. She couldn't say no, because she didn't want to say no. She looked at her feet for a moment, and when she looked back up—determined to tell Fran she was not going to Kay's—Fran was smiling.

"Hold on just a second," Fran said as she pulled her cell phone out of her purse and began dialing. She smiled again as she put the phone to her ear. "Hey, you'll never guess who I just ran into at the store."

Brenda wanted to walk away from her, but her legs didn't seem capable of cooperating with the rest of her body. Obviously, they were still listening to her heart, since it controlled the lower part of her body now, and not her head. As a result, she stood there silently and waited.

"Brenda," Fran said into the phone as Brenda looked in the other direction. "Yeah, I invited her to come along. I hope it's all right with you?"

Brenda began to wander at this point, but she felt Fran take her by the arm and hold her there. *What the hell am I doing?* She should just tell Fran she had to get home, and walk out of there. The problem was she *did* want to see Kay, no matter how much she tried to deny it.

When they were both finished in the store, Brenda agreed to follow Fran to Kay's house. She couldn't believe she was doing this, but she figured maybe it would be easier with Fran there too. At least nothing would happen with a chaperone in attendance, right?

It was after nine thirty when they arrived at Kay's, and she was waiting for them at the table out on the back deck. Fran had a key to the house, so she just let herself in. Brenda followed, and when they walked out to the deck and Kay turned to smile at her, she felt her heart skip a beat. She tried not to, but she couldn't help smiling back at her.

"Hey," Kay said, motioning to the bottles of beer in a bucket filled with ice. "Go ahead and help yourselves. There's plenty."

"I can only stay for one," Fran said as she smiled at Kay. Brenda didn't miss the wink she sent Kay's way either. She grabbed a beer and took the seat directly across from Kay. "Michael's plane landed a few minutes ago, so he should be home soon."

"How was your rehearsal?" Kay asked Brenda.

"Rehearsal for what?" Fran asked, looking at Brenda.

"I play the drums in a band," she answered. She shrugged and looked back at Kay. "It was all right, I guess."

"Where do you guys play?" Fran asked her. She appeared to be genuinely interested, but Brenda had the feeling Kay had already told her all about it.

"Discovery," Brenda answered before taking a drink of her beer.

"Where's that? I've never heard of it," Fran said. She looked at Kay. "Maybe we should go and see them play."

"No, it's a lesbian bar," Brenda warned her. She glanced at Kay who was just sitting there looking back and forth between them. It was obvious to Brenda she was enjoying this. Kay smiled at Brenda. "I'm not sure you'd be very comfortable there."

"Didn't Brenda do a wonderful job on the fence, Fran?" Kay asked, sensing Brenda wanted to change the subject.

"I might be able to comment on her workmanship if it wasn't so dark out here."

"Suffice it to say once the deck is finished tomorrow, no one will be able to see into the backyard." Kay turned her attention back to Brenda. "Thank you."

"No problem," Brenda answered.

"I should get going," Fran said as she stood. Kay smiled when she noticed Brenda still had more than half her beer left. Fran came and leaned down to kiss Kay on the cheek. "I'll show myself out and lock the door behind me. It was nice seeing you again, Brenda."

"You too," Brenda answered, watching her leave. When they were alone, she spoke to Kay again. "Look, I'm sorry about earlier."

"Don't be," Kay said reassuringly as she shook her head. "You have absolutely nothing to be sorry for. I should be the one apologizing. I know I can come on a bit strong sometimes."

"Okay then." Brenda smiled before finishing her beer. "I should be getting home. I've got to go to work in the morning."

"Please don't go," Kay said. She walked over to stand behind Brenda, setting another beer in front of her before her hands found Brenda's shoulders. "Stay and keep me company for a while."

Brenda flinched at her touch, but as Kay began to slowly massage her neck she could feel Brenda relax into her touch. Brenda untwisted the cap on her second beer.

"Is this okay?" Kay asked quietly, leaning down to speak into Brenda's ear.

"It's nice," Brenda said as Kay felt the shiver run through Brenda's body. Kay's hands began to work their way lower, but they were moving down Brenda's chest rather than her back. Brenda grasped her wrists and held them still. Her voice was choked. "I told you I couldn't do this, Kay."

"Can't? Or won't?" Just touching Brenda was turning her on. She wanted so badly to kiss her. To know if her lips were really as soft as they looked. But there was something holding her back. Something told Kay if she moved too fast with Brenda it would scare her away for good. She forced herself to pull her hands away and resumed her seat.

"Either or," Brenda said. She turned her head to look at Kay. "Take your pick."

"Why?" she asked. God, she wanted this woman. Wanted to know what it was like to hold her in her arms and to be held by Brenda's arms.

"We had this discussion already," Brenda reminded her.

"And just a few minutes ago, you apologized for earlier," Kay pointed out. "What were you apologizing for, exactly? I'm sorry if I misinterpreted what you meant."

Kay closed her eyes momentarily. The fire she felt was undeniable. The throbbing hum of arousal between her legs threatened to become all-consuming. She took a deep breath, opened her eyes, and reached over to take Brenda's hand, inordinately pleased when Brenda didn't pull away from her. As soon as their hands touched, it felt as if a bolt of electricity went through her.

"You have no idea what you're doing to me."

"I would imagine it's much the same as you're doing to me," Kay said, gently squeezing her fingers. She crossed her legs in an attempt to quell the itch she was feeling. "I don't know why I feel this way, but there's a connection between us, and I can tell by the way you look at me you feel it too. I want to kiss you, Brenda. Does that make me a horrible person?"

Brenda shook her head and smiled at Kay. She let go of her hand before getting to her feet. Kay did as well and took a step toward her.

"I need to leave now," Brenda said, almost whispering.

Leaving was the last thing Kay wanted her to do as they stood there looking into each other's eyes. She could see Brenda tense when Kay leaned toward her, but her lips only brushed Brenda's cheek.

"I'm sorry you feel that way," Kay said, turning to walk into the house. It was difficult to walk away from her, but there was no other option—at least not tonight. "Would you please reconsider having dinner with me some night?"

"I'll call you," Brenda answered. "That's all I can promise right now."

❖

Tommy Rayne sat in his darkened one-room apartment and stared blankly at the wall. The only light in the place was shining in from the streetlight outside. The bitch would pay for what she'd done to his nose. He made that promise to himself, and he intended to keep it.

There was no evidence linking him to those two dead women. He had seen to that. He'd always been able to clean up after himself. But the damn detective was like a dog with the proverbial bone. The cops were so sure they could find the evidence they needed, but Tommy smiled to himself. They'd never be able to find anything.

They thought following him would lead them somewhere new, but Tommy only went to the pawnshop and back home again. He rarely went anywhere else because they were watching him, but they didn't know *he* knew they were watching him.

He smiled as he thought about how he'd lost the tail earlier and driven by Griffith's house. He could have killed her and been done with it. Except the damn bitch from the bar had been sitting there in the middle of her driveway. He walked slowly to the bathroom.

He inspected his nose and was pleased to see the bruising around his eyes was finally fading.

And speaking of the dyke from the bar, why the hell was she riding him tonight? He knew she played in the band there, but he didn't know her name. She'd pissed him off too. But he'd deal with her later. First on his agenda was the fucking blond detective, Kay Griffith.

He'd kill her if it was the last thing he ever did. She'd made a comment about how ugly he was. He'd be the first to admit he wasn't the best looking guy in the world, but that wasn't anywhere near as bad as when she'd called him a worthless prick. He'd lost it then, because that was what his mother called him all his life. But she'd never call him that again, and neither would Kay Griffith.

He could be patient though, and he wasn't anywhere near as stupid as they thought he was. But he was content to let them think whatever they wanted about him. He'd bide his time and strike when they least expected it.

Yes, they'd soon find out Tommy Rayne was the most patient man in the world. He'd wait for his opportunity, and when it presented itself, he'd pounce, and she'd be his for the taking.

As he stood there looking in the mirror, his hands went to his back, between his shoulder blades, and he scratched furiously. It was a nervous habit he'd had forever, and his parents had even sent him to therapy to try to break him of it, but nothing seemed to work. He never even noticed he was doing it anymore—unless he was standing in front of a mirror.

He thought of the bitch Griffith again, and plotted in his mind how he'd kill her. It would be slow, that much he was sure of. Maybe a knife. He'd always liked knives. It seemed to be more personal that way. It was how he'd done those other two women. And it was how he'd done his mother too.

CHAPTER TEN

B renda chose to have her father help her finish Kay's deck. If her father was there, then maybe Kay wouldn't flirt with her. At least that's what Brenda was hoping. The ploy worked until late in the afternoon when her father went inside to use the bathroom. Kay apparently saw it as an opportunity to get Brenda alone.

"You've been avoiding me," she said. She nodded in approval as she looked at the deck they'd put in.

"I've been working." Brenda didn't even look up as she continued getting the hot tub reinstalled. Once that was done, all they had to do was clean up their tools and they'd be finished. She told herself she'd never have to see Kay again, but the thought didn't make her happy like she'd thought it would.

"I guess you're just about finished up, aren't you?"

"Yep. Another half hour at the most."

Brenda resisted the urge to look at Kay when she heard her sigh. She walked across the deck to get her bottle of water. As she took a drink, her eyes met Kay's and she almost choked. She wiped sweat from her forehead and knew she had to speak because the silence was deafening.

"I saw Tommy Rayne last night."

"You didn't talk to him, did you?" Kay seemed agitated at the news.

"Yeah, I did. I let him know I knew he had his nose broken by a woman. He wasn't very happy about it."

"Jesus, Brenda, stay away from him, all right?" Kay took a step toward her but then seemed to catch herself as she ran a hand though her hair. "Promise me. Trust me when I say you don't want Rayne to have you anywhere in his sights."

"I can handle him, Kay. Don't worry about it."

"He's a murderer, Brenda. Stay away from him."

"If he was a murderer he'd be in jail."

Kay walked over to her. Brenda felt her pulse quicken when Kay moved into her personal space. She made a conscious effort not to let on how Kay's close proximity affected her.

"Listen to me. Whether we ever see each other again or not, you need to keep your distance from him. We haven't been able to get any evidence on him yet, but do you remember those women whose body parts were found in different Dumpsters downtown?"

Brenda shifted her weight from one leg to the other and swallowed uncomfortably. She nodded her response. Of course she remembered it. When something so gruesome is all over the local news stations how could you forget it?

"I'm convinced it was him," Kay said after a moment. "I can feel it in my gut, Brenda."

"Are we about done here?" Brenda's father asked when he joined them on the deck. He went over to the hot tub without sparing them so much as a glance.

"Yeah," Brenda answered him without looking away from Kay. He may not have shown any outward sign of noticing how close they were to each other, but Brenda knew her father never missed a thing. There was no doubt she'd hear about it on the way back to the office. "You want to go ahead and start taking the tools back out to the truck? I'll finish up here."

He nodded before picking up a toolbox and disappearing back into the house. Brenda went back to check the connections for the hot tub. She could feel Kay's eyes on her as though she were actually touching her. She suppressed the shiver that caused goose bumps to break out on her arms.

"You've done a good job here, Brenda. Thank you."

Brenda finally looked up, but Kay was already walking into the house. She wished she could admit to Kay she was attracted to her. Kay had been honest with her the night before, but Brenda wasn't ready to put her heart out there again. It had been trampled too many times in the past for her to be so careless with it now.

❖

"I don't need to tell you it's not a good idea, do I?"

Brenda shook her head at her father's question but refused to look at him, instead choosing to watch the road in front of her. She heard him sigh and knew he was watching her. He'd keep staring at her until she acknowledged him with words.

"You don't have to worry about it, Dad."

"Really? Because that isn't how it looked when I walked back out there. I may not know much about being gay, but I sure as hell know lust when I see it."

"Jesus, Dad," Brenda murmured.

"What? Are you going to deny it?"

Deny it? Hell, yes. Right after she crawled under the nearest rock. Sometimes Brenda thought he embarrassed her on purpose just to get her to blush. She remembered the time she brought home a girl for the first time and he brought out all the baby pictures of her. She'd spent the evening sitting in the corner with her head in her hands as she listened to both her parents telling her date about all the crazy things she'd done when she was little.

"I don't need to deny anything. The job's done, and I'll never see her again."

He didn't say anything and she continued to stare at the road before her. After a few moments, he cleared his throat and she saw from the corner of her eye he was twisting in his seat to look at her.

"Getting involved with a client is never a good idea."

"No?" Brenda said, fighting the grin tugging at her lips. "Tell me again how you met Mom?"

"That's different."

"The hell it is. You were remodeling her parents' kitchen if I remember the story correctly. How many times did you ask her out before she finally gave in just to shut you up?"

"It was different," he said again. "She wasn't the client; her parents were."

"Semantics, Dad. If I told you it was Kay's parents who hired us, would that make it okay?"

Brenda realized her mistake too late. She seriously would have kicked herself if it had been physically possible.

"Kay, is it? Interesting. You can deny it all you want, Brenda, but I saw the way you both watched each other all day long."

"Like I said, the job is done. I have no reason to ever see her again, so don't worry about it, all right?"

He laughed, and Brenda finally took a moment to glance at him. She wondered what exactly he seemed to find so funny all of a sudden.

"I've never told you this before, because, well, let's face it, your mother and I never did like Janice or Nina. But if you take the two of them out of the mix, you have impeccable taste in women. I taught you well."

"Oh, my God, you were checking her out?"

"If you say a word to your mother I'll disown you. Don't think I won't."

They laughed together, and Brenda felt the tension leave her shoulders for the first time since they'd gotten in the truck to leave Kay's house. She was grateful every day she had such a close relationship with both her parents. She could talk to them about anything. And she knew without a doubt if she were to bring Kay home to meet them, they would be the ever gracious hosts they always were. Because underneath it all, Brenda knew they wanted to see her happy.

"Don't forget dinner Monday night at Dave and Buster's. I can't believe your mother would choose to have our anniversary dinner there."

"It's the video games. You know that, right?"

"No, she likes to see me make a fool of myself on Dance Dance Revolution. If that's the price I have to pay in order to make her happy, then I'm more than willing to do it."

"And if you have to spend a hundred dollars in order to collect enough tickets to win her a stuffed animal?"

"A small price to pay," he said with a wink. "Hey, maybe you should invite Ms. Griffith to come along to dinner with us."

"For God's sake, will you stop about her?"

"What does she do for a living?"

"She's in security," Brenda answered without hesitation. It wasn't truly a lie, but she'd told her parents she'd never get involved with another cop again. She didn't take the time to think about why she was lying about it since she was never going to see her again.

CHAPTER ELEVEN

The following Monday, when Brenda walked into the office to find all of their employees had shown up for work, she was pleasantly surprised. Would wonders never cease. She might have a chance to get some paperwork finished for a change. Since the night she ended up going to Kay's unexpectedly, she'd started carrying a change of clothes with her. Right now she was wearing khaki shorts and a tank top similar to the one she'd worn the first day she worked at Kay's.

Why was it Kay continued to creep into her thoughts? The day hadn't even started yet, for God's sake. She'd been happy to get that particular job finished though. She hadn't been able to stop thinking about Kay all weekend. Kay had been on her best behavior when Brenda's father was there with her. While Brenda would never admit it out loud, she enjoyed the attention Kay gave her when she flirted. After everything her last two girlfriends had done to rip apart her self-esteem, having a woman like Kay show an interest in her was an incredible ego booster.

"Grace, I do not want to be disturbed," she told the receptionist as she walked in with her obligatory twenty-four-ounce coffee. She was going to need it if she hoped to stay awake the entire day. Paperwork was the most boring job there was, but it had to get done. Hank was good for some of it, but she needed to take care of paying the bills.

"Not for anything?" Grace asked, smiling. She had been working for Jansen Construction for over ten years, and she and Hank were their most trusted employees.

"Use your best judgment," Brenda said with a smile of her own. "But if you disturb me because someone walks in off the street wanting to use the toilet, I won't hesitate to fire you."

Grace laughed and waved her away before she went back to answering the phones.

Brenda closed the door behind her and went to sit behind her father's big walnut desk. He'd taken the day off to celebrate his and her mother's anniversary. There was a large picture window facing the reception area, so the pretense of privacy in his office was comical at best. Her father had wanted it that way so he could keep an eye on everyone's comings and goings. She used his office when he wasn't there, because hers was in the warehouse where there was no air conditioning. August in Pennsylvania was not a good place to be with no air conditioning.

She proceeded to bury herself in the bills needing her attention. By noon, she had most of what she'd intended to do done. She leaned back in her chair and stretched her arms above her head as she glanced out at the reception area. She almost fell backward when she saw Kay walk in the front door and approach Grace's desk with a smile on her face.

Brenda watched in amusement when Grace shook her head at Kay, pointed toward Hank's office, which was also in the warehouse, and then Kay looked like she was pleading with Grace. At one point, Kay raised her eyes and caught sight of her watching them. A warm smile spread across Kay's face, and Brenda felt her heart speed up. She almost fell backward in her chair again. That slow, sexy smile was going to kill her yet.

Grace glanced over her shoulder at Brenda, and then picked up the phone to call her.

"There's a Ms. Kay Griffith here to see you, Ms. Jansen." Brenda almost laughed. Grace had *never* called her Ms. Jansen before.

"What is it in regards to?" Brenda asked, trying her best to sound professional. She could do it with very little difficulty with the suppliers and the customers, but she always had a problem acting this way with Grace.

"She would like to pay for the work you did at her house," Grace said. "I told her Hank could handle it for her, but she's insisting she needs to speak with you personally. Are you free to see her?"

"Yes," Brenda answered, but she wanted to say no. That wasn't entirely true. She really did want to say yes, but she didn't want Kay to know it. *Christ, I can't even think straight when it comes to her.* "Send her in."

Kay opened the office door a moment later and entered, then closed the door behind her. As she took a seat in front of the desk, Brenda saw Grace smiling and giving her the thumbs up signal before turning and going back to the phones. Brenda couldn't help but laugh.

Kay appeared a little confused as she looked over her shoulder at the reception area and then back at Brenda.

"Did I miss something?" she asked, her tone skeptical.

"Just Grace letting me know she approves," Brenda said. Damn, her mouth was always working faster than her brain when Kay was around.

"She approves?" Kay asked, smiling. "Of me?"

"Everyone is always trying to set me up with someone," Brenda explained to her. She couldn't look away from Kay's eyes. They were mesmerizing. "It seems as though everyone has a cousin, or a sister, or even the infamous friend of a friend they want me to go out with. But just so you know, no one has to approve of my choice in women. Only my opinion counts."

"And what is your opinion?" Kay asked as she leaned forward.

Wow, what a loaded question, Brenda thought. She wanted to tell her how much she wanted to kiss her, and would do it right here in this office if there had been no one else around.

But her mouth decided to stay closed. Kay smiled at her, waiting patiently.

"You really haven't been with anyone since…"

"Janice left me?" Brenda asked, and Kay nodded, obviously uncomfortable. Brenda smiled and was a bit surprised she was even willing to talk about it. "No, I haven't, but it's been by choice."

"Why is that?"

Brenda stared at her for a moment, wondering why Kay thought it was any of her business. Kay's gaze didn't waver in the least.

"What can I do for you?" Brenda finally asked, wanting to take care of whatever business Kay needed to discuss with her, but thinking in the back of her mind her words came across as a double entendre. She'd been hoping to ease the sexual tension that was so damned obvious between them. Grace must have noticed it as well, because she kept sneaking peeks over her shoulder. Brenda thought about closing the blinds, but my, oh my, wouldn't that set the tongues around the office wagging?

"I wanted to pay you for the work you did," Kay said, reaching into her pocket and pulling out cash.

"We would have sent you a bill."

"I was in the neighborhood."

"You were in a neighborhood forty miles from your house?"

"I wanted to see you," Kay finally admitted. "Is that what you wanted to hear?"

"Why do you keep flirting with me?"

"Because I find you incredibly attractive," Kay answered. They both continued to stare at each other. "And I would love to get to know you better."

"I could be an axe murderer."

"You could be, but I'm a cop. I'm pretty sure I could take care of myself."

"You just aren't going to give up, are you?"

"I will when you agree to go out with me." Kay sat back, her expression smug. Brenda couldn't help but chuckle and shake her head.

"Okay, fine. I'm having dinner at Dave and Buster's tonight. Would you like to join me?"

"Just the two of us?"

"Actually, no. There'll be another couple there." Brenda hoped the look on her face was just as smug as Kay's had been. She knew her parents wouldn't be too upset if she brought a date along to their anniversary dinner. After all, they were always pestering her to start dating again. Her father had been joking when he suggested she bring Kay to dinner, but Brenda saw it as a way to get rid of Kay. No doubt she'd be furious at meeting both her parents on their first—and probably last—date.

"A double date?" Kay seemed intrigued by the idea. She finally nodded. "What time should I pick you up?"

"I'll pick you up at seven, if that's okay with you."

"Perfect."

There was silence then, and it stretched out to the point it became uncomfortable as they continued to look at each other. Brenda felt her pulse quicken, and her chest was rising and falling a bit too rapidly. Shit, she'd forgotten she was wearing the tank top, and she noticed Kay's eyes keep falling to her chest. Brenda realized she didn't really mind it though. It was flattering.

"I have a lot of work to do," Brenda finally said, her voice sounding as though she were dying of thirst.

Kay nodded and stood before handing the money over to Brenda. Their fingers brushed when Brenda reached for it, and Kay sucked in a breath.

"If you want to wait a minute, I'll have Grace give you a receipt."

"No, I should go. You can bring it when you pick me up tonight. I'll see you at seven?"

"Yes."

Kay nodded and turned to leave, not trusting herself to stay any longer. Her desire to have Brenda in her arms was overwhelming. But if all went well on their date, Kay hoped she'd have her in her bed by the end of the night. She smiled pleasantly at Grace as she walked through the front office and took a deep breath when she was finally outside.

She crossed the parking lot to her car as she pulled her keys out of her pocket. Her steps slowed when she caught sight of an envelope tucked under the wiper on her windshield. There were two words written on it: *Detective Griffith.*

Kay looked both ways down the busy street but didn't see anyone walking. She briefly thought about calling Paul but finally shook her head and grabbed the envelope. She ripped it open and unfolded the single sheet of paper she'd pulled out of it. Her pulse pounded in her ears when she read what it said.

I'm watching you.

She stood staring at the words for what felt like an eternity before she heard someone calling her name. Kay turned to see the receptionist from Brenda's office—Grace—walking toward her.

"Is everything all right?"

"Did you see someone out here while I was inside?" Kay asked as she folded the note and shoved it into her back pocket.

"No, I'm sorry," Grace answered. "What's wrong?"

Kay forced a smile and waved her hand in dismissal. "Nothing. Someone left a note on my windshield but didn't sign their name. Not a big deal." Kay got into her car and started it, not wanting to get into a conversation about it, especially with a woman she didn't even know.

Tommy Rayne. Who else could it have been? She shook her head and pulled out of the parking lot. And why the hell was he following her?

Chapter Twelve

K ay let Max out about ten minutes before Brenda was due to arrive that evening. Unfortunately, he decided to pick then to show his stubborn streak and refused to come back in the house. She was out on the back deck trying to coax him in with a treat when the front doorbell rang.

"You stupid dog," she muttered as she made her way through the house. She pulled the door open and felt her frustrations with the dog melt away when her eyes met Brenda's. She stepped aside and motioned her in. "I'm locked in a battle of wills with Max. I want him to come inside, and he wants to piss me off."

Kay started walking back toward the kitchen just as Max started barking furiously. If she hadn't gotten the note on her car earlier she wouldn't have thought anything of it, but she reached up on top of the refrigerator and grabbed her weapon. After checking to make sure it was loaded, she slipped it behind her back into the waistband of her shorts.

"Max!" she yelled as she walked out onto the deck, but he wouldn't look at her. His attention was fixed on a part of the fence as far from the house as he could be. She watched while he sniffed at the fence and then started to dig. Kay turned to apologize to Brenda but was surprised when she found her only a few inches away. "I'll go get him. You wait here."

"Why do you need a gun?" Brenda seemed nervous.

"It's Philly." Kay shrugged as if those two words were all she needed by way of explanation, and unfortunately, it was. Maybe she would tell Brenda about the note, but then again, maybe she wouldn't. It all depended on how their date went. "I'll be right back."

She walked across the yard slowly, carefully listening for anything out of the ordinary. When she got halfway to the dog, she thought she heard someone running away, and then Max gave one last chuff before turning and trotting over to her, his hind end wiggling.

"Good boy, Max," she said while she scratched behind his ears. She was never so happy to have him as she was in that moment. Maybe it wasn't Rayne, but if it was, he'd now think twice before trying anything at her house again. She took one last look out there before closing the sliding glass door and securing it. She smiled when she turned back toward Brenda, who was being molested by one hundred and thirty pounds of Rottweiler. "He likes you. He didn't even warm up to Fran this quickly."

"He's a good boy," Brenda said in that voice people use when they're praising a dog, which only caused him to lick her face even more. She was crouched down and barely keeping herself from falling backward from his weight. She laughed as she petted him, and Kay's heart warmed at the sight. "Enough, Max. I'm taking your mommy out for dinner. Is that all right with you?"

Kay laughed when Max sat down but couldn't keep his butt still. His tongue was hanging out of his mouth as he alternated looking at Brenda and then Kay.

"He says it's fine as long as you bring him a doggy bag."

"I think I can arrange that." Brenda smiled, and she visibly relaxed for the first time since she'd walked through the door.

"So who are we meeting for dinner?"

"Just a couple celebrating their wedding anniversary," Brenda answered as she held the door to the restaurant open for Kay. She looked around the seating area and didn't see her parents. The hostess told her the rest of their party hadn't arrived yet, so she motioned for Kay to follow her to a small waiting area.

"Gay marriage isn't legal in Pennsylvania. Where were they married?"

"I'm sorry. Did I give the impression it was a gay or lesbian couple? It's not. They're straight. I hope that isn't a problem for you."

"No, some of my best friends are straight."

Brenda's breath caught in her throat at the smile Kay gave her. She did her best to not give away how Kay affected her, but she was pretty sure it was obvious.

"How long have they been married?"

"Thirty-seven years."

"Excuse me?"

"It's my parents."

"You're introducing me to your parents on our first date?" Kay began to pace, and Brenda thought for sure she was going to escape out the front doors. "Why would you do this to me? Jesus, I'm wearing shorts and a T-shirt, Brenda. To an anniversary dinner. For your parents."

"Relax. In case you haven't noticed, I'm dressed the same way. It was obvious to me you weren't going to give up on asking me out, so I decided why not?"

"What if they don't like me?"

"You already met my dad, and I'm pretty sure he thinks you're okay. As far as my mom is concerned, that might be a problem. She didn't like the last two women I got involved with, and I know now I should have listened to her about it," Brenda said. She took a seat and grabbed Kay's hand, pulling her down to sit next to her. Their bare legs touched and Brenda had to concentrate on not giving in to the jolt of desire it caused.

"Honestly, Kay, we don't even know if *we* like each other. I wouldn't worry too much about trying to impress my parents."

"Easy for you to say. I don't think you'd feel that way if we were here to meet my parents."

Brenda thought about it and had to agree. She'd probably be mad as hell if Kay had brought her to dinner with her parents, so why should she expect anything different from Kay?

"I'm sorry. You're absolutely right. I'll take you home if that's what you want." Brenda waited for an answer, but Kay's eyes were fixed on something behind her. Brenda looked over her shoulder and smiled when she saw her parents walking toward them. She hugged her mother. "Happy anniversary, Mom."

"Thank you, honey." Her mother kissed her on the cheek before releasing her and taking another step toward Kay. "Who's your friend, Brenda?"

Brenda glanced at her father who was obviously trying not to smile. He shook his head and focused his attention on the dining area.

"This is Kay Griffith," Brenda said as she went to stand by Kay's side. "Kay, these are my parents, Laura and Gary Jansen."

"It's a pleasure to meet you, Mr. and Mrs. Jansen," Kay said. Brenda was impressed her tone didn't give away any of the nervousness she knew Kay was experiencing.

"Oh, please," her mother said before pulling Kay in for a hug. "It's Laura and Gary, and I'm very happy to meet you, Kay."

The hostess led them to their table and took their drink orders before leaving them to look over the menu. There was no talk other than what sounded good to eat until after the waiter took their orders.

"So," Gary said after the waiter walked away from their table. He looked at Kay for a moment and then turned his attention to Brenda. "Does this mean you two are dating?"

Kay watched as Brenda shifted uncomfortably in her seat. She cleared her throat and smiled at the Jansens.

"We only met just last week."

"Then you're only friends." Laura's tone was unmistakably disappointed.

"Not if I have anything to say about it," Kay answered with what she hoped was a cheerful smile on her face. "I've asked Brenda to have dinner with me a couple of times, but she's refused my invitations. Today she finally gave in and asked me to join you all for dinner. I had no idea we were going to be dining with her parents."

The blush she saw creeping up Brenda's neck to her cheeks was incredibly endearing if not downright sexy. Kay forced herself to look away and concentrated on Laura, who was sitting across the table from her.

"What do you do for a living, Kay?" Laura asked.

"I'm a homicide detective." Kay regretted the words when she saw the pained expression on Brenda's face. If she wasn't supposed to tell them about her job, Brenda should have informed her ahead of time.

"You said she was in security," Gary said with a pointed look at Brenda.

"Well, it is security." Brenda looked away and swallowed audibly. "Sort of."

"So you're a cop?" Gary asked, his skepticism obvious. He looked at Brenda as though she'd lost her mind. "Are you kidding me? After what Janice put you through?"

"With all due respect, sir, Janice isn't a police officer," Kay said quickly. Kay wasn't sure why they all seemed to be anti-cop simply because Brenda's ex-lover worked at the police station. It irritated her when people assumed all cops were jerks just because of one bad experience.

"Maybe not, but she certainly slept with a lot of them," Laura said.

"Mom, Dad—"

"I'm not Janice," Kay said, interrupting Brenda's attempt to calm her parents. "And I can assure you I'm not one of the cops who slept with her. I'll be the first to admit I haven't known your daughter very long, but I hope to get to know her better. I've never cheated on anyone in my life, and I can promise you I never will. And honestly, cheating is something inherent to an individual, not a profession."

Kay could feel her temper rising and fought hard to keep it under control. The last thing she needed was to do something stupid in front of Brenda's parents. Brenda seemed to sense her growing anger and placed a hand firmly on her thigh just above her knee, squeezing gently.

"You remember reading about the cop who broke the nose of a murder suspect?" Brenda asked in what Kay was happy to recognize as an attempt to change the subject.

"I seem to recall something about it," Gary answered absently but never took his eyes off Kay. "The scumbag deserved it, if I remember right."

"Yeah, he did." Brenda glanced at Kay. "It was her. The detective who whacked Tommy Rayne across the face with the butt of her gun was Kay."

"Really?" he sounded unimpressed, but Kay saw a glimmer of respect in his eyes. He nodded once to indicate he was willing to give her another chance. "Good for you."

Kay nodded back, an acknowledgment of their momentary truce. She knew the gesture also meant if she ever hurt Brenda she'd have to answer to him. Kay looked at Brenda and thought there was no way she could ever hurt her, intentional or not.

CHAPTER THIRTEEN

I'm not sure your parents liked me very much," Kay said when Brenda pulled into her driveway a little after eleven.

"Honestly, I think they did." Brenda put the Durango in park but didn't cut the engine. She didn't know if Kay was going to invite her in or not, but she didn't want to assume anything. "They didn't demand you leave, did they?"

"That's the litmus test?" Kay asked with a grin. "I liked them, even if they didn't like me."

"You did?" Brenda asked.

"They love you. That much is obvious. And anyone who is so protective of their child gets my approval, so yeah, I liked them."

Brenda was relieved, but she wasn't sure why. At what point during the evening had it begun to matter whether Kay liked her parents and they liked her? It wasn't supposed to happen. She'd intended to take Kay along, expose her to the grilling she knew her parents would subject her to, and then revel in the fact Kay had no interest in seeing her again. But things hadn't worked out like she'd planned. Brenda found herself wondering what it might be like to wake up next to Kay.

"I had fun tonight," Brenda said quietly. She smiled when Kay held up the small teddy bear Brenda had given her. Usually, when she'd go to Dave and Buster's she never won enough tickets to get a prize any better than a plastic spider ring. But this night her parents had pooled their tickets with hers and talked her into getting the bear for Kay. It was impulsive, and crazy, and Kay had loved it.

"So did I." Kay turned her head and looked at the house as if she expected something to be out of place. To Brenda it looked exactly as it had when they'd left a few hours earlier. Kay smiled when she looked back at Brenda. "Would you like to come in for a cup of coffee?"

"I should go. I have to work in the morning." On some level, Brenda knew she was turning the ignition off as she spoke the words, but she didn't care. She wasn't ready for the evening to end yet.

"Okay, see? That was a contradiction. Your actions didn't match your words. I'm assuming that means you're coming in?"

Kay reached for the handle to open the door, but Brenda placed a hand on her wrist to stop her. When Kay turned back to look at her, Brenda's eyes were fixated on her lips. When Kay's tongue darted out to wet her lips, Brenda stifled a groan. Without giving much thought to her actions, Brenda leaned closer and placed a gentle kiss on Kay's mouth.

"What was that for?"

"I just wanted to get it out of the way. Now we don't have to deal with the awkward moment later of whether or not a good night kiss is appropriate."

Kay just smiled before getting out of the car and walking to the front door. Brenda followed wordlessly, so many thoughts flying through her mind at once. Kay turned her on; that much she couldn't deny. But given her past experience with relationships, she shouldn't be going into her house after their date. She should have dropped her off and driven home. Yet here she was, standing on Kay's front porch, waiting for her to open the door so they could go inside.

They made their way into the kitchen where Kay started a pot of coffee before letting Max out into the backyard. When he came back in, he went right to Brenda and shoved his nose into her hand, looking up at her with those eyes all dogs seemed to have. The ones that say, *I know you had steak for dinner. Where's mine?*

Kay laughed and opened the bag she'd set on the counter. When the aroma reached Max's nose, she looked at Brenda.

"Do you want to give it to him? You are the one who asked for the doggy bag."

Brenda nodded, not quite trusting herself to speak. She took the bag and reached in as Max sat in front of her panting and squirming. She held a piece of the meat for him, expecting him to be all teeth when he grabbed it, but he was surprisingly gentle as he took it from her fingers.

"Good boy," Brenda said. She laughed when he nudged her in the thigh with his nose, his eyes locked on the bag she still held. She looked at Kay.

"I know. I was surprised the first time I fed him from my hand too. I'm still amazed at how gentle he is."

They were silent as Brenda fed him the rest of the steak. When she was done, she washed her hands and joined Kay at the table, where she was sitting with two cups of coffee.

"Want to go in the hot tub?" Kay asked with a grin.

"I completely forgot to bring my suit."

"You don't need one."

Brenda thought about it, but shook her head. Getting into a hot tub with a naked Kay was not a good idea. Not if she wanted to take things slow and see if there really could be something between them.

"Thanks, but I'll have to pass this time."

"Perhaps a rain check then?"

"Maybe."

"That's as good of an answer as I'm going to get?"

"Right now, yes."

Kay nodded and they drank their coffee in silence for a few moments.

"Can I let him out?" Brenda asked when Max started whining. Kay nodded and Brenda stood to open the door for him. Before she could even think of pulling the door closed again, Kay was there, her arms going around Brenda's waist from behind. She leaned her head back, her eyes closed, and she let out a soft moan when Kay's lips touched her exposed neck.

Brenda knew she should put a stop to whatever it was Kay was trying to do, but damn, after a year of celibacy it felt good to be held by a woman again. When Kay's mouth moved to her ear, Brenda almost melted in her arms.

"You feel so good, Brenda," Kay said, her voice causing an uncontrollable shiver to run through Brenda. "So fucking good."

Brenda's chest was rising and falling rapidly, but she took a deep breath in an attempt to calm her thundering heart before turning in Kay's arms and taking a step away from her. She shook her head.

"This isn't going to happen, Kay." Brenda knew her body's reaction to Kay belied her words, but she felt she needed to be honest with her.

"This?" Kay asked, looking confused.

"You and me. It isn't going to happen."

"Tonight? Or ever?"

Brenda didn't know what to say. She was attracted to Kay. Who wouldn't be? She'd be lying if she tried to tell Kay she didn't want to sleep with her, and she knew Kay would know it was a lie. She swallowed and shook her head.

"Definitely not tonight."

"So you're saying it *could* happen sometime in the future then?" Kay smiled, and Brenda couldn't help it—she laughed. "Because I'm good with that, you know. We can take things as slow as you need. I'm not going anywhere."

"No, you don't understand."

"Then help me to." Kay took her hand and led her back to the table.

"I have a habit of jumping into things too quickly. Relationships, I mean." Brenda knew it was an understatement, but she hoped it explained things sufficiently. She'd been in bed with Janice only a couple hours after meeting her. Janice moved into her apartment less than a week later. With Nina it had been pretty much the same. Neither relationship turned out well, and Brenda had decided—with Dana's help, of course—she would take things slow with the next woman she thought might be relationship material. "Things tend to end badly when I rush into things like that."

"Okay," Kay said, looking confused. "Like I said though, we can take things slow. As slow as you need to take it. I can be old-fashioned if it's what you need from me."

Brenda tried to tamp down the incredible rush of excitement. If Kay was willing to move at the pace Brenda set, then maybe her love life could finally work the way she wanted it to. With Janice and Nina, *they* were the ones who set the pace. Brenda went along because she allowed herself to be ruled by her libido. If she could manage to rein in her sexual desire and move slow with Kay...

"You expected me to throw you out, didn't you?" Kay asked with a serious tone. When Brenda didn't answer right away, Kay began to worry. "Wait—you don't *want* me to throw you out, do you?"

"No," Brenda answered with a slow smile. "What I want is to take my time getting to know you. You've made it pretty clear you're interested in me, and it would be so easy to dive right in with my eyes closed. With my track record, it can only be a good thing if we move slowly."

"Look, I know Janice cheated on you," Kay said. She really didn't know Janice outside of work, but right then, seeing how gun-shy Brenda was, Kay hated Janice. She hated her for even thinking of hurting Brenda, and if she was there now, Kay knew she'd do to Janice what she'd done to Tommy Rayne.

"It wasn't just her." Brenda sat back in her chair and wouldn't make eye contact. "Nina was before her, and the same thing happened."

Kay had no clue what to say. She tried to gather her thoughts while she waited patiently for Brenda to look at her. When she finally did, Kay reached across the table and took her hand.

"I won't insult you by pointing out I'm not either one of them." Kay spoke quietly and maintained eye contact with her. She wanted Brenda to know she was being sincere in what she was saying. "But I can promise you I would *never* cheat on you. It's just not how I'm wired. The women in your past are just that—in your past. Please don't use the things they did to judge me because I will treat you the way you deserve to be treated. All I ask is for you to give me a chance."

When she saw Brenda's eyes fill with tears, Kay went and knelt by her side. The last thing she wanted was to make her cry. Brenda must have seen it in her eyes.

"It's okay," she said, one hand on Kay's cheek. Kay leaned into the touch slightly. "Your words made me happy, not sad."

"Good," Kay said, relieved. "And I meant every word I said. I hope someday you'll know it to be true."

"I should probably be getting home," Brenda said after a moment.

Kay held a hand out to her, helping her up. When they were both on their feet, Kay rested her hands on Brenda's hips, wanting to kiss her, but not knowing if it would be welcome or not.

"I know you already kissed me to get it out of the way, but it was a rather platonic kiss. So is kissing allowed?" she finally asked. "Because if you say no, I'll probably combust right here in front of you."

"Yes, kissing is allowed." Brenda laughed and put her arms around Kay's shoulders, pulling her closer. "In fact, if you don't kiss me, I may start to doubt the things you said to me."

"We can't have that, can we?" Kay's smile faltered when she felt a surge of arousal at the sight of Brenda's tongue wetting her lips. She closed the short distance between them, and their lips met at the same time as their bodies. Brenda's arms held her close and she melted into the kiss, sweet and chaste at first, but then more heated when Brenda's tongue skimmed along her lips. She moaned deep in her throat when her tongue slid along Brenda's, and her hands searched for a way under Brenda's shirt.

After a moment of fumbling like a teenager, she pulled away and tried to catch her breath. Brenda's eyes were still closed and they stood with their foreheads touching and their breath mingling as they both struggled to breathe normally.

"Holy fuck," Brenda said. "If this is how you always kiss, I may need to rethink the whole going slow thing. Your mouth is amazing."

"You should leave before I try and take you up on that." Kay pulled away reluctantly, acutely aware of the loss of contact between them. She forced a smile, trying not to let on how totally wrecked she was after their kiss. Somehow she managed to walk Brenda to the door as if everything was perfectly fine when it was anything but. Her body was on fire with need, and Kay knew going slow with Brenda might just kill her. She stopped Brenda with a hand to her forearm as they reached the door. "When can I see you again?"

"Tomorrow?"

"Here, for dinner? How does seven work for you?"

"Perfect. I'll see you then."

Kay stood in the doorway watching while Brenda got into her truck and drove away. When she couldn't see the taillights any longer, she shut the door and locked it before turning on the alarm. She stopped on her way back to the kitchen, and an icy fear gripped her when she heard Max barking and scratching frantically at the sliding glass door.

"Max!" she yelled, but he kept on barking and snarling. She walked slowly into the kitchen, her attention fixed on the dog. After grabbing her weapon, she went to him and turned the lights on outside. She quickly scanned the yard but saw nothing.

Max finally stopped barking and was now alternating between growling and whining. She scratched his head absently before pulling the blinds closed and urging him to follow her upstairs. Between the thought of Rayne stalking her and the way her body was still keyed up after kissing Brenda, she knew it was going to be a long night.

Chapter Fourteen

Tommy's heart was racing as he scrambled over the fence. The fucking dog was really starting to piss him off. He hated dogs—especially Rottweilers. They were nothing but overgrown testosterone-laden freaks as far as he was concerned. Maybe he could catch the dog outside someday and toss it a raw steak. Then while it was busy eating it, he could put a bullet in the back of its head. He smiled at the thought.

He almost laughed when he thought about Griffith kissing that other woman. He *knew* she was a dyke. That was the thing that set her off the day she broke his nose. It had to have been.

"Hit a little too close to home, didn't I, Detective?" he said under his breath. He leaned his head back against the fence and gazed at the stars. In the city, you couldn't see the stars because of all the lights, but here on the main line it was a little easier. Still not as good as somewhere out in the country, but Tommy would take what he could get.

He looked through one of the slats in the fence and could see Griffith at the sliding glass door looking out into the yard.

"Don't worry, bitch," he said. "You'll get yours soon enough. And I'll enjoy the hell out of giving it to you."

He waited for a good hour after she turned out all the lights before moving from his hiding spot. If she was watching for him, he didn't want to give her the satisfaction of knowing it was him. Better to let her squirm a bit. He walked the two blocks to where he'd left his car. The cops were following him, and they didn't even try to hide it. He'd lost them when he stopped by the pawnshop and borrowed Billy's car. The kid wasn't too bright, but he always did everything Tommy told him to do. They didn't even notice him sneaking out the back door and driving away. It was Griffith who had the hard-on for him. The rest of them were pretty lax in keeping tabs on him. *She* would be more vigilant about watching his every move, but with the restraining order, she couldn't get anywhere near him. He smiled at his reflection in the rearview mirror before pulling away from the curb and heading back downtown.

"I'm telling you, Paul, it's him. It has to be."

"Griff, you admitted yourself it's dark in the backyard. How could you possibly be certain it was him you saw?"

"Because I'd know the little scumbag anywhere. Who else could it have been?" Kay was pacing in her bedroom, all the curtains drawn tight. Max was on the foot of the bed whining as he watched her. Once in a while she'd stop and scratch behind his ears in a weak attempt to reassure him—or maybe she was trying to reassure herself—and he'd tentatively wiggle his butt. She'd stood at the window behind the closed curtains, all the lights off, waiting for someone to move in the yard. She'd been about to give up and go to bed when she saw a head pop up from behind the fence at the far end of the yard. Kay didn't hesitate to call Paul even though it was after midnight. "The bastard has a restraining order against me. He needs to stay the hell away. If you won't talk to his lawyer, then I will. And if he leaves any more notes on my windshield—"

"What?" Paul said. She could hear him getting out of bed. His wife's muffled voice was in the background, and he murmured something to her and there was silence. After a moment, he was back on the line. "Why the fuck didn't I know about any notes he left you?"

"I was going to tell you tomorrow," she said, taking a seat next to Max. He promptly lay down and rested his chin on her thigh. "It was late this afternoon, and I had a date tonight."

"Remind me to ask you about it later, but I want to know why you didn't call me, or Quinn, for that matter, the second you found the note. Jesus, Kay, if Rayne's violating his own restraining order, then we need to know."

"I know. And I'll bring you the note first thing in the morning, I promise. But I know it was him in my yard tonight. *Twice*. There's no one else it could have been. This dog doesn't go ballistic like that for no reason."

They hung up after arranging for a time to meet, and Kay tossed the phone onto the bed behind her. She rested her hand on Max's head and looked into his eyes. If she was going to pursue anything with Brenda, she had to let her know about this. It would only be fair to let her know what kind of fucked up situation she might be getting herself into.

CHAPTER FIFTEEN

After meeting with Paul, Kay stopped at the store to buy the ingredients she needed to make dinner for Brenda. She pulled into the driveway a little after three. She stopped when she saw a manila envelope leaning against her screen door. She set the bags down and picked it up, her heart pounding at the now familiar handwriting.

Detective Griffith

For a moment, she thought about not opening it at all. The smart thing to do would be to turn around and take it to Paul, but she shook her head. Kay hated feeling helpless, and she hated having to turn to someone else for protection. She tucked the envelope under her arm and grabbed the bags before walking into the house.

Paul informed her the uniforms assigned to tail Rayne the night before claimed he was in the pawnshop all evening. She didn't buy it, and neither did Paul. Kay knew surveillance was a shitty job, and she also knew suspects could be extremely inventive in the art of shaking a tail. Rayne was no stranger to police procedure. She had no doubt he was a good little boy and did nothing but travel between work and home, but when he had something he needed to do without someone watching over him, he could probably lose them without much effort.

She went through the preparations for making lasagna and had it in the oven before she finally took a deep breath and sat at the table with the still unopened envelope in front of her. They'd dusted the other one for prints but they'd only found hers. If Rayne was their killer, there was no way he'd be so careful in leaving no evidence on the bodies just to leave an errant fingerprint on an envelope. That was the rationale she used for not delivering it to Paul right away.

She turned it over in her hands a couple of times before finally opening it. Her breath caught at the photo of her and Brenda kissing in her kitchen the previous night. A tremendous feeling of being violated came over her before all conscious thought ceased, and she felt nothing but fury as she came to the realization Rayne really was stalking her. She flipped the photo over and read the chilling message.

She's cute, Detective. I'd hate to see anything bad happen to her.

Her first instinct was to rip the photo to shreds, but she finally flung it away from her before trying to calm her racing pulse. She had to tell Brenda about this. It wouldn't be fair not to. But she was worried Brenda would never want to see her again, and she wasn't sure she could handle that kind of rejection.

At exactly seven, her front doorbell rang and she couldn't stop her hands from shaking. Max helped to call attention away from her by bounding to the door and greeting Brenda the second it was opened.

"Hey, Max," Brenda said before laughing and kneeling to accept a kiss or two. When she looked up at Kay, Kay couldn't help but smile at her dog's exuberance. "Hey."

"Hey yourself," Kay answered. She grabbed Max's collar and pulled him back so Brenda could enter the house. Brenda closed the door behind her as she held out a bottle of wine.

"I hope it goes with whatever you're fixing for dinner."

"It's perfect." Kay took the Malbec and motioned for Brenda to follow her to the kitchen. She poured them both a glass and handed one to Brenda. "Dinner can wait for a few minutes. There's something I need to talk to you about."

"Okay," Brenda said, the trepidation evident in her tone. "Are you breaking up with me already?"

"No, but *you* might want to after we talk."

Kay led her to the living room and they sat next to each other on the couch. Brenda was watching her with obvious concern, and Kay closed her eyes for a moment. This wasn't going to be easy.

"I know you said you usually do remodels and such, but I thought maybe you could refer someone. I need to have some security lights installed in the backyard. You know, the kind that go on when it senses motion."

"Is this about what happened last night before we went to dinner? When you went out there with your gun?"

"Yes." Kay wanted to leave it at that, but she couldn't. "Remember the last day you were here to work and I asked you to stay away from Tommy Rayne? He's stalking me. And he knows about you."

Max walked into the room, his tongue hanging out, and sat next to Kay. She scratched behind his ear and he stretched his head out to rest his chin on her thigh.

"I don't understand," Brenda said. "What do you mean he *knows* about me?"

Kay could feel Brenda's eyes on her as she pulled out the photo. She didn't hand it to Brenda right away, but instead put it face down on the coffee table. She knew because the handwriting was so small, there was no way Brenda would be able read it from where she was sitting. And even if she could, the words would have no meaning without having seen the photo.

"Yesterday when I was at your office, he left a note on my windshield. This morning I took it to Paul, my lieutenant. We're pretty sure it was him, but there weren't any fingerprints on the paper. When I got home, there was an envelope at my front door with this inside." Kay finally handed the photo to Brenda before she lost her nerve.

Brenda stared at the photo of the two of them kissing in the kitchen the night before. Her pulse quickened at the thought of what could have happened to Kay when she'd gone out to the yard with her gun. A chill ran down her spine as she fought to not let panic set in. She almost lost the battle when she turned it over to read the short message on the back.

"He's been watching us?" Brenda's voice sounded strained to her own ears.

"Apparently. Now do you understand why I want you to stay clear of him?"

Brenda only nodded, not trusting she could speak without her voice giving away how frightened she was. The fear of being involved with a cop overwhelmed her. Janice had only gone to crime scenes after the horror was over, but Kay, being a detective, would be placing herself in danger every day on the job. She'd never worried about Janice being hurt, or even worse while she was working, but with Kay it was a real possibility.

"I'll understand if you want to leave and not see me anymore," Kay said as if she could read her mind. Brenda met her eyes and saw her own fear reflected there.

"Is that what you want?"

"No." Kay spoke quietly but without hesitation. "But it isn't fair for me to expect you to put yourself in danger. He's a murderer, and we *will* find the evidence to get him convicted. The problem is things are moving at a snail's pace."

"If I stopped seeing you do you think I would be in less danger? Because if he wants to get to you, he could still do it by hurting me." Brenda realized then she'd already made up her mind. She wasn't about to let a third party control her life, which was something her parents taught her. *She* was in control of her life, and there wasn't anyone who could dictate what she could or couldn't do. Besides, she'd probably be safer with a cop than by herself, right?

"No, I don't," Kay said, her shoulders relaxing slightly.

"I don't know where this might lead, but I'm not about to let some asshole take it away before we can find out." Brenda looked around the room to make sure all the curtains were drawn before standing and offering her hand to help Kay up. When they were both standing, Brenda moved into her personal space and placed her hands on Kay's hips. "I think we're supposed to have dinner, right?"

"In a minute," Kay said before touching Brenda's cheek with her fingers and closing the short distance between them to kiss her.

Brenda opened her mouth when Kay's tongue sought entrance. She gave in to the sensations and heard herself moan when Kay's hand moved down her neck and shoulder to cup a breast. When she lightly squeezed Brenda's already hard nipple, Brenda broke the kiss and took a step away from her.

"Dinner now, before I give in."

Kay smiled before taking her hand and leading her to the kitchen. When they were seated with plates full of lasagna and garlic bread, Kay reached across the table and took Brenda's hand.

"So can you refer someone to install the security lights for me? The sooner the better."

"I'll be here first thing in the morning to do it myself," Brenda said before taking a bite of the lasagna and closing her eyes at the wonderful taste. Kay could definitely cook.

"I didn't expect you to do it."

"I'm a certified electrician, and I want to do it. Why should I let someone else do it and possibly screw the job up when there's so much at stake? I'll make sure it's done right."

Brenda didn't take the time to think about how her words sounded, but she was incredibly pleased at the look of gratitude on Kay's face. Her smile didn't even falter when she realized she'd do almost anything to make Kay happy.

❖

Tommy scratched between his shoulder blades with both hands as he watched the two uniformed officers walking through his shop. He hadn't wanted to be there tonight, but it was Billy's night off. Griffith would just have to spend the evening without him. He wondered if her new girlfriend was with her again tonight, and he wished he could have seen their faces when they saw the photo he'd left for them.

He looked out the front door and saw the surveillance team was still out there, about a block away. The two uniforms were either a coincidence, or they were stepping things up in the wake of his gifts to Griffith. He'd have to back off on that for a while.

He resisted the urge to check the rear door to the shop to see if there were more cops waiting out there for him to try to get away from them. He found it comical they were spending so much time watching him, because there was no way in hell he'd ever let them see him do anything wrong.

"Can I help you gentlemen find anything?" he asked as he approached the officers.

"No, we're just looking," one of them said with a smile.

"Take your time. I'll be here all night."

He returned to the counter and took a seat once again, watching intently as the two officers spoke quietly to each other. Let them waste their time. He'd find the perfect moment to make his move, and when he did, they'd all be scrambling to figure out how he'd managed to do it.

CHAPTER SIXTEEN

A re you okay with things the way they've been?" Brenda asked one night after they'd gone to dinner and a movie. They'd been dating for almost two weeks and were standing in the kitchen of Brenda's small apartment, Kay's arms around Brenda's waist from behind. Kay's chin was resting on Brenda's shoulder as they waited for the coffee to finish brewing.

"What do you mean?" Kay asked.

"I know things have probably moved a lot slower than you ever thought they would." Brenda covered Kay's hands on her stomach with her own. "I want to thank you for being so patient with me."

"I want to thank *you* for allowing me to get to know you before we confuse everything with sex." Kay turned her head and kissed Brenda below her ear. "I like you a lot more than any other woman I've ever been with, and we haven't even slept together yet."

Brenda turned in her arms and settled her ass against the counter. She could see the sincerity in Kay's eyes, and she felt a lump form in her throat.

"Really?"

"Really." Kay gave her a chaste kiss on the lips before moving away from her and leaning against the refrigerator, her arms crossed over her chest. She had a crooked smile Brenda was beginning to find incredibly sexy.

"You're amazing."

"How so?" Kay asked.

"You're so confident and sure of yourself."

"That's how you see me?"

"Yeah." Brenda nodded. "Why? You don't?"

Kay shook her head and looked away. Brenda wanted to go to her and gather her up in her arms because she looked so lost all of a sudden. Something held her back though. Something told her Kay needed a moment to gather her thoughts. Just when she thought she should probably change the subject, Kay looked at her again.

"I'm anything *but* confident and sure of myself," she said. "I'll admit I'm better than I used to be, thanks to the love and nurturing my uncle Norm gave me. I wish you could have met him. The two of you would've liked each other."

"He sounds like an amazing man," Brenda said.

"He was." Kay smiled. "He helped me to see who I am. Growing up, I never felt like I belonged anywhere, so I kept trying to figure it out. I went to an all-girl Catholic school, and I sure as hell didn't belong there. And my family? I *really* didn't belong there. I was a disappointment to my parents, especially when I became a police officer, and the final straw was coming out to them. I haven't spoken to them in ten years. When they told me I was an abomination and would burn in hell, I made the decision to cut them out of my life."

"I can't imagine what that would be like," Brenda said, silently thanking whoever was responsible for her parents being so accepting.

"No, you're lucky. Your parents love you unconditionally, as it should be. But even now, as an adult, I'm sometimes not sure where I belong." Kay shrugged as she smiled at Brenda. "For the most part things are good at work. Paul is my biggest fan, and then there's my partner, Quinn. Becker and Elam are okay too, but Colley and Porter? I could definitely do without them."

"Why?"

"They're misogynist assholes." Kay chuckled in what appeared to be an attempt to hide her hatred for Colley and Porter, but Brenda knew she wasn't doing it because it was humorous. "Women need to be told what to do, how to act, when to speak. Serious cavemen attitudes."

"It sucks to have to put up with that day after day," Brenda said. She knew she was lucky. Being a woman in a typical man's profession, she could easily have encountered the same chauvinism. She gained the respect of the other guys by having to do twice as much work. She had the feeling though that with the two Kay was talking about, nothing would ever change their views concerning women.

"I'm thinking about resigning," Kay said.

"What?" Brenda was surprised, but she tried not to show it. The elation she felt made no sense since they were still getting to know each other. "Why?"

"A lot of reasons." Kay shrugged. "Cases like this one with Rayne are especially taxing, because no matter how much I try and do things the right way, he gets away with *everything*. And then a freaking judge grants him a restraining order against me. How fucked up is that?"

"It's pretty fucked up," Brenda agreed. She shifted her weight from one foot to the other as she contemplated whether to ask if this had anything to do with Brenda not wanting to be involved with a cop. But it would be crazy considering they'd known each other for all of two weeks, wouldn't it?

"I started seriously thinking about it three years ago," Kay continued, almost as if she could read Brenda's mind. "Long before this case. But with Rayne? We had him, Brenda. There was a rape victim who identified him as her attacker. We had him dead to rights. And then she recanted. Paul told me the morning Rayne had been released, and I went right to his shop. The woman refused to talk to us anymore, and the case was dropped. I feel like I'm not making the difference I'd hoped I would when I decided to join the force."

"What would you do if you did resign?"

"I don't know. I haven't thought very far ahead. With the money Uncle Norm left me, I could go to school for something, and I wouldn't have to work for quite a while."

"What did Norm do for a living?" Brenda couldn't help but think talking about the not so pleasant things in their lives was a much better way to truly get to know one another. She was falling for Kay, big time. And it was because of the things she shared with her like she just had. With sex off the table they were less guarded in their conversation topics. They were more or less just friends spending time together. Brenda's opinion was you tended to talk to friends about things you'd never tell your lover. You wanted to be perfect for your partner, especially in the beginning of the relationship, but your friends knew everything about you. The good and the bad. And even the ugly, for that matter.

"I don't know," Kay said with a shake of her head. "I'm pretty sure it was probably illegal though. He always had money and never hesitated to help people out when they needed it, including the brother who despised him."

"Your father?"

Kay nodded before she pulled out a couple of coffee cups from the cupboard and filled them both. She rested a hip on the counter and faced Brenda. "Enough of this. We're on a date, right? So let's talk about upbeat things."

Kay let Brenda take her by the hand and lead her out to the living room. She wasn't sure why she'd become so chatty this evening. She hadn't even told Fran she was thinking about leaving her job.

"I shouldn't stay long," Kay said. She'd only been to Brenda's apartment once before, but she knew to look out for the errant spring in the couch. She sat on the other end of it and left that spot for Brenda. "Max will need to go out soon. I don't want him to start using my furniture as his personal bathroom area."

"I can certainly understand that," Brenda replied with a nod. She put her coffee cup on the table and scooted closer to Kay.

Kay sucked in a breath and put her cup down as well. Brenda placed her hand on Kay's thigh, which sent a delectable shiver up Kay's spine. "Are you cold?"

"No," Kay answered. Brenda didn't usually initiate their physical contact, and Kay found herself hoping it meant they were closer to sharing more. She covered Brenda's hand with her own and squeezed it gently. With her other hand, she touched Brenda's cheek before running her fingers through her hair. She could seriously get lost in those eyes. "Kiss me, please."

Kay's arms went around her neck as she pulled Brenda down on top of her. She spread her legs so Brenda could settle between them and then wrapped them around her, pressing her center hard into Brenda's pelvis. Their tongues slid easily against each other, and Kay moaned into her mouth. After a moment, Brenda lifted herself up with her hands.

"You said you couldn't stay long," Brenda reminded her, and Kay closed her eyes in an attempt to block out her responsibilities. It didn't work.

"I should go," she said, not wanting to release Brenda, but knowing she had to. When Brenda was on her feet, she held a hand out to help Kay up. "I don't want to go."

"I know. I have rehearsal tomorrow night, and then we're performing on Friday. Can I see you Saturday?"

"Absolutely," Kay answered. She was a little disappointed Brenda had never invited her to watch the band play, but she figured Brenda needed something to be just for her. Until she was invited, she would stay away from the club. She should stay away regardless since Rayne's shop was right next door to Discovery. All she needed was for somebody to report her for violating the restraining order. She gave Brenda one more quick kiss before heading for the door. "See you Saturday."

When she was in her car, she rested her forehead against the steering wheel and sighed. She felt like a damned teenager letting herself get all worked up just to be told no. She wasn't sure how much longer she could take it. She met her eyes in the rearview mirror and laughed.

"Like hell, Griff. You'll take it for as long as it takes." She shook her head and started the engine. She was beginning to fall for Brenda Jansen, and she wasn't entirely sure when it had happened.

CHAPTER SEVENTEEN

To Kay, the next few weeks seemed to both crawl by and pass way too quickly. Her time with Brenda seemed to fly by, but she was tired of waiting out her suspension. And the shrink—God, how she hated those appointments. She made sure to tell him everything he wanted to hear. Yes, she was remorseful for having assaulted a man. Yes, she was working on getting her temper under control. No, she would never allow anything like that to happen again.

He must have believed everything she said because he'd cleared her to return to work on Monday. That meant she only had three more days to see Brenda whenever she wanted to. She wasn't at all sure she even wanted to return to work.

They'd spent a lot of time together, but Brenda was still taking things slow. It was sweet torture to be with her, whether they were out to dinner or at a movie. The most torturous though was sitting on the couch watching movies at home. Brenda seemed to be content falling into a routine, but Kay was always left wanting at the end of their time together. They were constantly touching, whether thigh to thigh or holding hands, and more than once Kay had fallen asleep with her head in Brenda's lap, waking to the feel of Brenda's fingers gently combing through her hair. And their make-out sessions on the couch would no doubt make a teenager blush.

She couldn't deny something felt very right about getting to know each other before jumping into bed together, but it was exhausting kissing and touching only to be left hard and wet with her own hand the only way of finding any relief.

The good thing was Tommy Rayne seemed to have fallen off the face of the earth. He was still around of course, but Kay hadn't received any more notes or photos from him. Quinn reported that Rayne had been on his best behavior since the night of her first date with Brenda. They hadn't found anything to bring him in on, and according to Quinn, the lieutenant was close to pulling the surveillance on him. Not because he wanted to, but apparently the captain was getting on his case about using manpower for a "pointless investigation."

"How are things going with Brenda?" Fran asked when Kay opened the front door to let her in. She kissed Kay on the cheek before heading to the kitchen without waiting for an answer.

"The same," Kay said. Fran poured them both a cup of coffee before they settled in at the kitchen table.

"I'm worried about you, Kay. It's not like you to be seeing someone for this long and you haven't slept together yet."

"It's been nice, Fran. I know more about her than I've ever known about any other woman, and I *still* want to sleep with her. That's got to be a good thing, right?"

"If you say so. All I know is if I wanted someone so badly and was denied physical satisfaction for so long, I'd be seriously reconsidering things." She searched Kay's face, but Kay couldn't meet her gaze. Fran smiled knowingly. "You're falling for her, aren't you?"

"I don't know. Maybe," Kay said with a shrug. She certainly couldn't deny it. Brenda made her feel things she'd never felt before. "So what if I am?"

"I can play *what if*. What if she never wants to have sex?"

"I don't think that's going to happen," Kay said, but how could she be sure? The thought had crossed her mind on occasion, but the way Brenda reacted to her touch told her the celibacy wouldn't last forever.

"Okay, then what if it isn't worth the wait? What if you sleep with her and then decide you don't want to see her anymore?"

"What if it's the best sex I've ever had in my life? What if I realize I can't live without her?" Kay sighed in exasperation. "We can play this game all day, but it won't solve anything. All I know is right now, I want to spend time with her. I want to continue getting to know her. I'm *not* going to sit here and think of all the negative things that could happen."

"Fair enough. So tell me why you've never gone to listen to her band play?"

"She hasn't asked me to. I want to give her her space, and showing up there uninvited seems presumptuous."

It wasn't as though Kay hadn't thought about going to the bar one night to watch her play, but it seemed to her it was Brenda's way to blow off steam, and she hadn't wanted to intrude. She did want to let her have her space, but it was getting harder and harder with each passing day to keep her distance.

"You need to invite her to come see you play," Dana said as she and Brenda were walking to the car on Thursday night after their rehearsal. "Are you ever going to introduce me to her, or is she some hideous creature you're embarrassed to be seen with? Ooh, maybe you're afraid she'll fall for me and leave you in the dust."

"God, you're a pain in the ass," Brenda said with a laugh. She looked over her shoulder and saw Tommy Rayne watching them from the doorway of his shop. She'd noticed him paying way too much attention to her over the past few weeks, but she wasn't about to worry Kay by mentioning it to her. She got into the Durango and pulled her phone out of her pocket as Dana closed the passenger door. "I'll call and invite her to come tomorrow night. Will that make you happy?"

"Immensely." Dana clapped her hands like a little kid who'd finally gotten her way, and Brenda couldn't help but laugh at her.

"Hello," Kay said in Brenda's ear. As usual, Brenda's pulse spiked just at the sound of her voice.

"Hey, beautiful," Brenda said, ignoring Dana's heckling. "I just got done with rehearsal and wanted to hear your voice."

"Jesus, Brenda, you drive me crazy. Why don't you come over?"

"As tempting as it sounds, I can't tonight because I have an early morning meeting with one of our suppliers." Brenda tried to banish the thoughts of what might happen were she to take Kay up on her offer. It was definitely getting harder to stay celibate. She knew she would give it up very soon, but she didn't want it to be on a night when she had to be up early the next day. She intended to take her time exploring Kay's body. "I was calling to invite you to Discovery tomorrow night to watch us play."

"Then you didn't call just to hear my voice?" Kay's tone was teasing, and Brenda chuckled.

"Can't I have more than one reason to call?"

"Of course you can, baby. And I'd love to see you play. What time should I be there?"

"We start at nine, so just don't be late."

"I wouldn't dream of it. I'll see you tomorrow then."

"Sweet dreams, beautiful," Brenda said. She smiled when she heard a quick intake of breath from the other end of the line.

"You have no idea what you do to me."

"Maybe you can show me tomorrow night." Brenda knew how her words would be taken, and she admitted it was time. Time to show Kay exactly how much she'd come to care about her. Before Kay had a chance to respond, Brenda ended the call and shoved the phone back into her pocket.

"Did I just hear you tell her you're going to have sex with her tomorrow night?" Dana asked.

"Maybe." Brenda started the SUV without even a glance at her.

"It's about fucking time. I was beginning to think you weren't ever going to sleep with her."

"I'm pretty sure she was starting to think the same thing."

CHAPTER EIGHTEEN

Kay tried her best to hurry Fran across the street to Discovery. She had seen Tommy Rayne coming out of his shop and hoped to God he wouldn't spot her. Why hadn't they just gotten there a little later? Or earlier, even? She was beginning to wonder why she'd given in when Fran insisted on tagging along. If the night was headed where she hoped it was—where Brenda's suggestive phone call the night before indicated it would go—she didn't want Fran hanging around. At least she'd had the foresight to make Fran drive. That way, if Brenda *did* want to spend the night with her, they wouldn't have to drive two cars.

"Hey, you fucking bitch!" she heard Rayne call out. Fran stopped to turn around.

"Come on, let's just keep going," Kay pleaded quietly, a hand on her elbow in an attempt to get Fran moving again. "Ignore him."

"What's the matter? You're not so tough when your partner isn't around to back you up?" he called out. His hands went behind his head and began scratching feverishly between his shoulder blades.

"That's him?" Fran asked, but she still wouldn't move, despite Kay's plea to do so. Kay nodded, and Fran looked as if she were going to yell back at him. Kay yanked on her arm hard enough to force her to move and practically dragged her into the bar where the band was already playing. "What an ugly little man. Why doesn't he wear an eye patch, for God's sake? He'd even repulse a blind person."

"Because he doesn't give a shit about what anyone thinks of him," Kay said. "And I don't want to spend the evening thinking about him. I have other things on my mind tonight."

"I'm sure you do." Fran grinned at her as Kay paid the cover charge for them both.

"Get your mind out of the gutter."

"What the hell was that thing he was doing?" Fran asked as they made their way to a table near the front. She put her hands behind her neck and simulated scratching between her shoulder blades. It appeared she wasn't quite ready to drop the subject of Tommy Rayne. "Was he scratching? Does the man have fleas?"

"Honestly, it wouldn't surprise me if he did. I don't think the man's showered since nineteen eighty-three." Kay pulled out a chair and sat, her eyes meeting Brenda's almost immediately. She smiled when Brenda nodded once in her direction before turning her concentration back to her drums.

"So has the mystery woman shown up yet?" Dana asked as they made their way to the bar when they ended the first set.

"She's here," Brenda said. The bartender, Carol, started to get her a soda, which was Brenda's usual choice while they were playing, but Brenda shook her head adamantly before reaching across the bar to grab Carol's arm. She proceeded to order a beer.

She'd never been much of a drinker, but she'd been nervous as hell since the phone call the night before. She knew without a doubt where this night was headed, and she was ready for it. The problem was she'd never been this nervous about sleeping with a woman before. She was worried after making Kay wait so long she might disappoint her. And truth be told, it was the reason she was still stalling after almost a month. Brenda hoped the beer might help to calm her nerves.

"What the hell are you doing?" Dana asked, indicating the bottle Carol handed Brenda. "Have you forgotten you aren't able to hold your liquor?" She leaned in closer, obviously having only asked the question as a courtesy. She was smiling a bit devilishly as she discreetly scanned the crowd. "Where is she?"

Brenda didn't need to answer, because Kay was already standing there behind her, and Brenda somehow knew it without even turning around. Her skin tingled and she felt a fluttering deep in her belly.

"Hello," Kay said, briefly touching Brenda on the shoulder. She smiled at Dana, and extended a hand in greeting. "You have a very nice voice."

"Thanks," Dana answered, not even trying to hide the fact she was checking Kay out. Even without turning around to see Kay, Brenda was able to watch as Dana's eyes went from Kay's legs to her eyes, pausing for a bit too long at Kay's breasts. "I'm Dana."

"Kay," she replied, her mouth close to Brenda's ear. Brenda found herself wishing their gig was over and she could be alone with Kay. The past few weeks had taken its toll on her physically, and she wanted nothing more than to have Kay under her—naked. Kay backed away from her, and Brenda felt a chill at the loss of her body heat.

"I've gotta pee," Dana said, leaning in close so only Brenda could hear. Brenda just nodded and swallowed hard. "Girlfriend, if you don't take advantage of this, then I'll take her home with me."

When Dana had started to walk away, Brenda fully turned to face Kay. Her heart was racing wildly, and she felt a little dizzy. The perfume Kay was wearing made her want to bury her face in the cleavage Kay had on display.

"Just so there's no misunderstanding, I have no desire to go home with Dana." Kay smiled.

"Neither do I," Brenda said. When Kay tilted her head to one side, Brenda felt her cheeks flush as she realized how her words must have sounded. "I mean, I don't want you to go home with her either. I mean, I don't want to go home with her—"

"I know what you meant." Kay seemed to take pity on her and slid a hand down Brenda's arm before entwining their fingers and squeezing gently.

"Did Fran come here with you?" A lame attempt to change the subject, but Brenda felt her heart slowing as she concentrated on taking even breaths.

Kay looked over her shoulder to where Fran was sitting watching them. She seemed to be a little too interested in what was happening between them. Kay moved so she was blocking her view, her back to Fran.

"We rode here together, if that's what you mean."

"Her car or yours?"

"Hers. I figured it would be easier. In case you wanted to do something when you're done here. That way I could ride with you and not have to worry about her getting home safely."

"Smart thinking." Brenda nodded and swallowed most of her beer in one gulp. She was finally beginning to regain her composure.

"Would you like to do something when you're finished here?"

Brenda only nodded before facing the bar and finishing what was left in the bottle. She motioned for the bartender to bring her another one. She thought for a moment she was seriously close to spontaneously combusting.

"You're kind of cute when you're nervous," Kay said, her mouth close enough to Brenda's ear she could feel her breath on her cheek. She put her hands on Brenda's hips and lightly pressed her pelvis against Brenda's ass. When Brenda leaned back into her, she heard a sharp intake of breath and Kay took a step back. "Come dance with me."

"I'm not sure that's a good idea right now," Brenda said with a shake of her head.

"I'll dance with you, honey," said a woman from behind them. Brenda turned to face a woman who was sporting a crew cut. Rita was friendly enough, but Brenda had always seemed to rub her the wrong way. As a result, they usually steered clear of each other.

"Back off, Rita," Brenda told her, trying to sound friendly, but, to her own ears, she sounded a bit possessive. She realized she felt possessive too. She didn't want Kay to dance with Rita, or with anyone else for that matter.

"Hey, the lady wants to dance." Rita smiled with a shrug and tried to move a little closer to Kay, who in turn pressed her hip against Brenda's. "If you're not willing to oblige her, I will."

"No, thank you," Kay said with a pleasant enough smile. She slid an arm around Brenda's waist and pulled her closer. Brenda was pleased to discover Kay seemed to be in a possessive mood as well.

"What's the matter? I'm not good enough for you, honey?" Rita asked. She feigned being hurt, but Brenda knew it was all an act. Rita came on to everyone at one point or another, and she usually ended up taking someone home, so if she were to be shot down now, it wouldn't slow her down one bit. She'd just move on to the next unsuspecting woman.

"She's with me, Rita," Brenda said as she put her arm around Kay's shoulders and took a drink of her beer before setting the bottle back on the bar. "And if the lady wants to dance, then I will dance with her."

They walked toward the dance floor just as a slow song began to play. Kay's arms went immediately around her waist, and she was looking into Brenda's eyes as Brenda's arms went around Kay's neck. Kay rested her head on her shoulder, her lips close to Brenda's ear.

Kay took a chance and kissed Brenda right below her ear. Brenda moaned quietly, but not so quiet Kay didn't hear it. Kay smiled and let her body sway with the rhythm of the music.

"I want to go home with you tonight," Brenda said.

Kay leaned back and her breath hitched at the look of pure desire in Brenda's eyes. She felt her own growing arousal between her legs when she noticed the flush on Brenda's neck.

"You are so damned sexy," Kay said, one hand on Brenda's cheek.

Brenda didn't answer, but instead closed her eyes as Kay slowly moved her hips against hers. Brenda leaned in to kiss Kay's neck as Kay moved her hands to Brenda's shoulders. She didn't care if they were in a room full of people. All that mattered was Brenda, and the way she felt in her arms.

"I want to make love to you, Brenda," she said when she found Brenda's ear again. Brenda responded by moving her hands up Kay's back, but she never stopped kissing her neck. "I want you so much; I don't know how much longer I can hold back."

Brenda finally moved to Kay's ear and bit the lobe gently, causing Kay to jerk involuntarily against her. Kay turned in her arms so her back was pressed against Brenda, who responded by putting her hands on the fronts of Kay's thighs and slowly pulling her hands up to rest on her hips.

Kay leaned her head back on her shoulder, and she closed her eyes as she felt behind her for Brenda's hips. Once she had her hands where she wanted them, Brenda's hands moved to cover hers, and her lips found a sensitive spot on Kay's neck. They moved together like that for the rest of the song. When it ended, Kay turned in her arms again to look into Brenda's eyes.

"When will you be done here?"

"Not nearly soon enough." Brenda was breathing heavily, and Kay was happy to realize she wasn't the only one who was completely turned on by their dance.

Kay stepped back and took Brenda's hand, lifting it to her mouth and smiling at her as she brushed her lips across Brenda's knuckles.

"I'll be waiting right over there." She pointed at the table where Fran was sitting, watching them with wide eyes. Kay thought she could almost feel Brenda's eyes on her ass as she walked back to the table.

"Oh, my God, that was so freaking hot," Fran said to her when Kay sat down. She leaned over and grabbed Kay's arm, squeezing it tightly. "I know I'm straight, but it was really, really hot. The way you two were touching each other, and moving? *I'm* turned on, so I know you have to be." She fanned herself exaggeratedly with the drink menu from the table. "Michael will be one happy boy when I get home tonight."

"Way too much information, Fran. I'm not sure I like knowing Brenda and I are fuel for your fantasies."

"How have you survived these past weeks if what I just saw was an indication of how you two spend your time?"

"She's coming home with me tonight," Kay said, unable to tear her eyes from Brenda, who was now making her way back to the bar with Dana. When she lost her in the crowd, she finally looked down at the table and tried to calm her thundering heart.

"So that's why you made me drive." Fran nodded and took a drink of her vodka tonic. "You're smarter than I give you credit for, sweetie."

"We're all going back to my place after this," Dana told Brenda as they stood at the bar, but Brenda was staring at Kay, and her breathing was a little rapid. Dana leaned over and spoke into her ear. "I caught the tail end of what was going on out there. I think the two of you turned the heat up in this place a few degrees."

"I'm going home with Kay," Brenda said. She wasn't paying attention to what Dana was saying. "You'll have to get someone else to give you a ride home tonight."

Dana didn't respond, so Brenda managed to tear her eyes away from Kay and turned to look at Dana. She had such a goofy look on her face Brenda couldn't help but laugh at her.

"I'm so happy for you, Bren," she said with genuine delight. She hugged Brenda tightly. "It's about fucking time you get back in the saddle. And she is pretty damn hot, if I do say so myself. You'd better enjoy yourself tonight."

"Oh, I intend to," she murmured as they went back to finish out their second and final set. Brenda wasn't at all sure how she was going to manage to get through the next hour.

CHAPTER NINETEEN

Brenda pulled into the driveway and was amazed she'd managed to keep her hands to herself for the ride home. Causing an accident wasn't on her agenda for the night though, so she'd sat there staring out the windshield for most of the ride. They walked into the house in silence, and after Kay locked the door behind them, Brenda reached for her in the darkness.

"Do you mind if I take a quick shower?" Kay asked quietly as she squeezed her hand gently.

"Not at all," Brenda answered.

"You're welcome to join me," Kay said as she led her up the stairs.

"I'm afraid it wouldn't be very quick then." She smiled as Kay turned the bedroom light on.

"You won't hear me complain."

Kay didn't object when Brenda turned to face her and slowly began unbuttoning her blouse. She could feel her own pulse raging wildly in her neck, and she suddenly felt very flushed. She almost melted when her hands went to Kay's shoulders under her blouse and eased it off. She hadn't felt this way since her first time with a woman in college. She was uncharacteristically nervous as she reached behind Kay to release her bra. Kay touched Brenda's cheek hesitantly.

"Are you sure you're ready for this?" Kay whispered.

"Why? Are you having second thoughts?"

"No, never. I just know you wanted to go slow, so I want to make sure you aren't going to regret this in the morning."

"I don't think I could *ever* regret making love with you." Brenda was staring at Kay's breasts and felt her knees almost give out as she watched her nipples tighten. When Kay placed a finger under her chin and forced her to look up, Brenda smiled sheepishly, her cheeks heating rapidly. "And besides, don't you think we've gone slow enough? I mean, what's it been? Four weeks?"

"Four and a half, but who's counting?" Kay shrugged as she reached down to unbutton Brenda's pants, her fingers dancing lightly over Brenda's skin.

"You are so beautiful," Brenda said. She ran her hands slowly up Kay's sides to her breasts, her thumbs brushing lightly over the taut nipples. She took hold of Kay's wrists and moved them away from her pants before proceeding to unfasten them herself. Kay's light touch was going to drive her mad. "Why don't you go start the shower? I'll be right there."

Kay nodded and disappeared into the bathroom. Brenda quickly removed her clothes, and then, for just an instant, she toyed with the idea of getting dressed and running out the front door. She couldn't do it though. It had gone too far for running away. She wanted Kay. No, that wasn't quite right—she *needed* Kay. Brenda was certain she couldn't function normally if she didn't sleep with Kay. The past four and a half weeks—and yes, she *had* been counting—had been so very hard, and there was no way she could walk away from Kay now. She couldn't even remember what her life had been like before she'd started spending so much time with her. If she were being honest with herself, she didn't want to remember.

Kay was already in the shower so Brenda pulled back the curtain and slipped in behind her. She pressed herself against Kay and felt Kay push back into her. Brenda smiled as she slipped her arms around her and cupped her breasts, squeezing them gently while she kissed Kay's shoulder before slowly running her tongue up her neck until she reached Kay's ear. She grasped the fleshy lobe lightly between her teeth, causing Kay to moan in pleasure, and then Kay's head dropped back against her shoulder.

Kay shuddered against her when Brenda moved her hands down her torso, and then one went right back to her breast as the other found the heat between Kay's legs. Kay jerked in her arms and moaned loudly when Brenda's fingers found her clit and began to gently massage it. The fingers on Brenda's other hand were methodically squeezing her nipple.

"So incredibly beautiful," Brenda said.

Brenda moved her hips with Kay's as Kay leaned forward and placed her palms on the shower wall. She moved against Brenda's hand in increasingly frantic thrusts. Brenda could tell she was close, but she didn't want Kay's first orgasm with her to be in the shower. She moved her mouth to Kay's ear before closing her eyes when Kay began to moan loudly.

"Tell me what you want," she whispered, breathing heavily. "Tell me what you want me to do to you."

"I want you to make me come," Kay told her between gasps. "Oh, Jesus, I want to feel you inside me. I *need* you everywhere, baby."

Brenda stopped what she was doing and reached down to turn the water off. Kay turned to face her with a look of worry Brenda interpreted to mean she thought Brenda had changed her mind about what they were doing. She kissed her, gently and passionately all at the same time in the hopes of quelling her fear, and Kay's arms went immediately around her waist.

They both dried off quickly and then Brenda took her by the hand to lead her to the bed. Kay lay down, pulling Brenda down on top of her, gasping loudly as Brenda's firm thigh went between her legs, and pressed hard against her center.

Holding herself up on one hand, Brenda ran her fingers slowly down Kay's cheek, and she smiled when Kay shuddered beneath her and closed her eyes. Brenda allowed her fingers to move lightly down Kay's body, around her breasts, and down her torso. She was delighting in the fact Kay's body was reacting so wonderfully to her touch.

"So freaking beautiful," Brenda whispered before taking a nipple between her lips and sucking lightly. Kay was urging Brenda to move down further, but Brenda took her time, enjoying the way Kay's hips jerked when she would bite down gently on her nipples.

Kay's hands went to Brenda's hips, her breathing erratic as she realized she was finally going to have Brenda the way she wanted so badly. She was still trying to urge Brenda lower, needing her to make her come, but Brenda took hold of one of her wrists.

"I need you to touch me," Brenda whispered in her ear as she took Kay's hand and slid it between her legs. Brenda gasped at her touch, and her hips moved forward to meet her hand.

Kay moaned when she felt how incredibly wet Brenda was. Her fingers gently squeezed her engorged clit, and Brenda bucked against her hand before pulling away and resting her forehead against Kay's shoulder.

"Careful, baby," she said, her voice raspy with need. "I'd hate to be done before we even get started."

She kissed Kay hungrily, and Kay felt her temperature rise when their tongues met. She didn't object when Brenda moved her mouth down and ran her tongue along Kay's neck to her breasts and continued on down her torso. Kay gasped loudly when Brenda's tongue began to explore between her legs. Kay's legs fell open further as Brenda's fingers gently squeezed her nipple, and her tongue found her clit.

"God...Brenda," she gasped as she arched her back when she felt Brenda's fingers slip easily inside her. Within moments, she was screaming out as the orgasm started deep in her belly before exploding up her spine. She tried to squeeze her legs together—tried to get Brenda to stop—but then before she knew what was happening, she was coming all over again. The ecstasy was too much, and she finally managed to force Brenda to crawl back up and lay beside her.

Her lips sought out Brenda's in the darkness, and she could taste her own passion on Brenda's tongue, which caused her sex to convulse as her body relived her orgasms. Kay was out of breath, and held tightly to Brenda, her fingers digging into her shoulders. But Brenda didn't complain, and her arms around Kay felt so nice. They kissed while Kay's body recovered from the pleasure Brenda had given her.

"You are fucking incredible," she murmured into Brenda's ear. She laughed softly. "I don't think I've ever felt so amazing in my life."

"It takes two," Brenda said as she kissed her forehead and then gently ran her fingers through Kay's hair. She gave her one of those slow, lazy smiles. "Why Tigger?"

"What?" Kay couldn't comprehend the seemingly out of the blue question.

"Your tattoo," Brenda said. "Why Tigger?"

"One night at the academy a bunch of us went out drinking." Kay hadn't thought about it in what seemed like forever. She chuckled as she told the story. "We decided to get tattoos. I was terrified of how bad it was going to hurt, so I picked the smallest one they had. It doesn't hurt that he's my favorite Disney character either."

"Did it hurt a lot?"

"Why? You want to get one too?" Kay kissed her forehead when Brenda just shook her head. "It didn't hurt nearly as bad as I thought it was going to."

"I think it's kind of sexy," Brenda said, her eyes moving slowly down Kay's body.

"Your turn," Kay said as she forced Brenda onto her back. The way Brenda looked at her made her even wetter than she already was. "I want you so much, Brenda."

Brenda moaned when Kay lowered her weight on top of her. She kissed Kay's neck and her hands moved over Kay's back as

Kay took a nipple into her mouth. She gently sucked and moved her tongue delicately around it. When Kay moved down further, Brenda's hands went to her sides and she grabbed the sheet, clenching it tightly in her fists.

Kay's tongue found its destination at the same time her fingers entered her, and Brenda's body jerked in response to her touch. She tried desperately to make the feeling last, but Brenda's body had other ideas. When the orgasm hit her, Brenda jerked upright, and she yelled out Kay's name. Kay continued to lap up her juices, relishing in the sweet, tangy taste of her until Brenda grabbed her by the upper arms and pulled her closer. They shared a passionate kiss as Brenda pulled Kay back down on top of her.

"Wow," Brenda said. "Just—wow."

"That good, huh?" Kay asked with a grin.

"Better," Brenda said, her eyes still closed. "I don't know the words to describe it."

"I'll take it as a compliment then."

"Definitely a compliment." Brenda tightened her hold on her, and Kay's last thought before drifting off to sleep was she could stay there on top of her forever.

CHAPTER TWENTY

The phone rang at two thirty in the morning, and Kay was instantly awake thanks to years of dealing with middle of the night calls. Brenda's head was resting on Kay's shoulder, and Kay's arm was firmly around her, holding her in place. Kay cursed when she realized it was her cell phone.

Her *work* phone.

Brenda sat up, and Kay kissed her cheek before swinging her feet over the edge of the bed. The phone was in her pants, which were still on the bathroom floor where she'd discarded them the night before. When she finally found the phone, she headed back to the bed and sat down.

"Griffith," she said. She ran her fingers through her hair and did her best to stifle a yawn.

"Kay, it's me," her lieutenant said. What the hell was he doing up this time of the morning? Better yet, what was he doing calling her this time of morning when she wasn't officially off suspension until Monday? "Sorry about the time."

"What is it, Paul?" she asked. She felt Brenda move behind her, and then she felt Brenda's hand on her hip. She smiled.

"Becker just called me," he said, referring to another detective from their unit. "Were you at Rayne's pawnshop earlier tonight?"

"What?" she asked in disbelief.

"You know you're supposed to stay away from him, Kay," Paul said. He sounded as if he was angry. "Becker and Colley saw you there tonight. What the hell are you thinking?"

"I wasn't there, Paul, at least not to see him," she said. Her free hand wandered over to cover Brenda's, and she held it tightly. "I was at the bar next door to see a friend who was playing in a band there. I happened to arrive as Rayne was closing his shop. I hardly even looked at him."

"You didn't say anything at all to him?" Paul asked. "You're sure?"

"Yes, I'm sure," she answered. "He was yelling shit at me, but I just ignored him. I was with another friend who wanted to rip him a new asshole, but I behaved myself."

"Good," Paul said, sounding immensely relieved. "That's the way Becker told it to me too. Colley's story was a little more damning though."

"Dale Colley's had it in for me since day one, Paul, and you know it. He'd say anything if he thought it could get my suspension extended. What did he say?"

"It's not important," Paul said before he sighed, and then there was a long pause. "He said you were yelling obscenities at Rayne and your friend had to hold you back. He said it looked to him like you would have killed Rayne if you'd had half a chance."

Kay worked hard at keeping her temper under control. Most of the detectives in homicide treated her like one of the guys. Dale Colley and his buddy John Porter were the exceptions. They didn't like the idea of a woman being in their ranks, and they didn't try very hard to hide their disdain for her.

"You know I don't believe him, Kay. I just wanted to hear your side of it, because you know the little weasel is going to tell his lawyer about it, and his story will probably be more in line with Colley's. This could cause a lot of grief for both you and the department. Please just promise me you'll stay away from that area until this all blows over, will you?"

"Until it all blows over? Don't you mean until Rayne trips up and we arrest his ass for murder?" Kay inhaled sharply when Brenda moved closer to her and kissed her near the base of her spine.

"Yes, that's exactly what I mean." There was another pause, and she heard Paul laughing softly. "This friend of yours who plays in the band, she wouldn't happen to be there with you now, would she?"

Kay turned and leaned down to kiss Brenda's cheek. "Yes, Paul, she is, so I'm sure you'll understand when I tell you I have to go now."

"Good night, Kay," he said, laughing. He hung up without waiting for her to respond.

"Sorry about that," Kay said as she crawled back under the sheet and pulled Brenda's body tightly next to hers once again.

"Not a problem as long as you don't have to go anywhere," Brenda assured her, taking one nipple into her mouth and squeezing the other between her thumb and forefinger. Kay moaned in pleasure as she lifted Brenda's face so she could kiss her.

"Will you be able to go back to sleep?"

"Not sure," Brenda mumbled, her lips moving down Kay's torso while her fingers still played with a nipple. "Probably not while I'm this turned on."

"Then we should take care of that." Kay closed her eyes and placed her hands on the sides of Brenda's face, her hips undulating slowly when she felt Brenda's tongue run the length of her sex. "Fuck…yes."

"Trust me, I intend to."

❖

Kay awoke at ten the next morning, and Brenda was still sound asleep. She managed to somehow untangle their limbs and carefully got out of the bed without waking her up. She pulled the sheet up over Brenda before placing a tender kiss on her forehead. Brenda let out a sleepy moan as she curled up tighter, seeming to be reaching for Kay. Kay smiled. She'd never felt better in her life.

Following a quick shower, she pulled on a pair of shorts and a T-shirt. After making sure Brenda was still asleep, she made her way down the stairs toward the kitchen for some much needed coffee. When she reached the last step, her cell phone rang. A glance at the screen told her it was Paul so she answered and put it to her ear.

"Griffith," she said as she entered the kitchen.

"We lost him, Kay," Paul said. He sounded incredibly uneasy.

"How the hell could you lose him?" she asked. "I thought there were units assigned to his house and his pawnshop."

"There were, but he lost the unit trailing him, and then he never went home last night. He didn't show up to open his store this morning either. Obviously, he has people working for him, but he always opens in the mornings. It's almost as if he's vanished into thin air."

Kay sat at the kitchen table and rested her elbows on her knees. She was beginning to think all hell broke loose when she wasn't around. They should've had enough evidence to bring Rayne in by now. Jesus, her suspension was up and now he was gone.

"What are you thinking, Paul?" she asked quietly.

"I'm thinking he may be coming after you," he answered, echoing what was going through her own mind. "I want to get you to a secure location, just until we can locate him again. There's an unmarked vehicle outside your house as we speak."

"Jesus, Paul," she said as she went to the living room to take a quick peek out the window. She saw Ryan Elam's vehicle on the other side of the street. The car was far enough away so as not to be obvious, but it still made her uneasy. "I'm not going anywhere. If it will make you feel better to have someone watch my house, then I can't stop you, but I'm staying here. I'll be back at work on Monday, and he isn't going to screw up my life any more than he already has."

"It would make me feel a hell of a lot better if I knew you were somewhere safe," he said. He hesitated and then let out a sigh. "Fine. You can stay there, but if he does show up, we're moving you."

"Okay," she agreed reluctantly before returning to the kitchen. "Thanks for caring, Paul. I'll see you Monday."

She ended the call and set the phone on the counter before getting the coffee pot ready. As she waited for it to finish brewing, she smiled again as her thoughts turned to the previous night with Brenda. It had been even more amazing than she had imagined it would be.

There wasn't much doubt in her mind about how she felt about Brenda. Fran's assessment was a little off. She *had* fallen for her. Hard. Everything seemed to be more in focus this morning. Her senses seemed to be heightened, and her heart felt lighter than it had in years.

She poured herself a cup of coffee and grabbed the cordless phone before letting Max out to the backyard, and she sat at the table on the deck. Not two minutes had passed when the house phone rang. She picked it up quickly, hoping it hadn't woken Brenda up.

"Hello."

"Is she still there?" Fran asked, barely able to hide her enthusiasm.

"She's still asleep in my bed," Kay answered, smiling. She was beginning to wonder if the smile would ever leave her lips. She hoped not. She liked the way it felt. She took a sip of her coffee.

"Sooo," Fran said, drawing the word out. When Kay didn't respond, she sounded a bit annoyed as she was forced to finish her question. "How was it?"

"You don't expect me to kiss and tell, do you?" Kay took another sip of her coffee and crossed her legs, enjoying the frustration she knew Fran was experiencing.

"Come on, I don't want to hear all of the sordid details, but at least tell me if it was all you hoped it would be. That it was worth the wait."

"Definitely worth the wait," was all Kay said. She heard a noise behind her and turned to see Brenda walking out onto the deck, her hair combed back and still wet from the shower. "She's up now, so I have to go."

Kay disconnected the call and smiled at Brenda, who was walking toward her.

"Good morning," she said.

"Yes, it certainly is," Brenda said as she leaned down to kiss Kay's cheek. She held up the cup she was carrying. "I hope you don't mind, but I helped myself to coffee and a shower."

"I don't mind at all." Kay studied Brenda's profile as Brenda watched Max playing with a tennis ball in the yard. The feeling of contentment surprised her a bit, but she liked it. Brenda seemed to settle her in ways no one else ever had. Kay felt she was right where she was supposed to be. When Brenda caught her staring, she didn't look away. Max ran up onto the deck and dropped his ball at Brenda's feet. She picked it up and threw it for him before turning her attention to Kay once again.

"If you keep staring at me like that I might have no choice but to drag you back upstairs."

"Trust me when I say there would be no dragging. I'd probably beat you back to the bed." Kay was amazed to feel the excitement growing deep in her belly. They'd stayed up most of the night exploring each other's body. There was no way she should be ready for more so soon.

"Is that a dare?" Brenda grinned. "You want to race?"

"There are so many things I want to do." Kay pushed her chair back and stood. When Brenda looked like she was about to stand also, Kay placed a hand on her shoulder and straddled her lap. "But racing is definitely not one of them."

She kissed Brenda, her hips pressing forward when Brenda's hands went under her shirt and moved slowly up her sides. The exquisite pressure caused from the seam of her shorts against her overly sensitive clit caused a gasp and she pulled away from the kiss.

"Fuck, baby, I'm gonna come," she said, unable to stop the thrust of her hips as Brenda squeezed her nipples. Right before she was about to go over the edge, her cell phone rang.

"Son of a bitch," Brenda muttered, her breathing as ragged as Kay's. "Ignore it."

"I can't. It's work." Kay forced her hips to stop moving as she fumbled for the phone on the table next to her. After doing her best to control her breathing, she answered. "Griffith."

"It's Paul. I'm just pulling into your driveway, so let me in when I get to the front door."

He hung up without another word and Kay wanted to scream. She tossed the phone back onto the table and ran her fingers through her hair before placing her hands on Brenda's cheeks and giving her a quick kiss on the lips.

"Do me a favor and hold that thought. We have company."

"You're so close though. Make them wait at the front door."

"I'd like nothing better than to lock myself away in the bedroom with you, but this can't wait. It's my job."

Brenda's demeanor changed in a heartbeat. She stood, almost dumping Kay on her ass, grabbed her coffee cup, and went back into the house just as the doorbell rang. When Kay made it into the kitchen, she grabbed Brenda's arm and turned her so they were facing each other.

"What the hell, Brenda? What did I do?"

"This is why I swore I'd never get involved with a cop. These past few weeks it was so easy to forget about your job because you were out on suspension. But now that you're going back to work, I'll never be any better than second on your list of priorities. No matter what time of day or night, when they call, you'll be out the door"

"That isn't true, baby," Kay said, unable to stop the feeling everything was about to slip away from her. "Please, just listen to me. This is about Tommy Rayne, all right? He lost his tail last night, and nobody's seen him since. Brenda, you could never be anything but my number one priority. Please give me the opportunity to prove it to you."

The doorbell rang again, followed by loud and impatient knocking. Kay glanced toward the front door and Brenda pulled her arm away.

"You'd better answer it."

"Promise me you won't leave. We need to talk about this when Paul's gone again."

Kay waited for Brenda to nod her agreement before walking to the door and pulling it open, certain both her anger and frustration were evident. She was surprised to see Quinn standing next to Paul on her front porch. Not that she thought otherwise, but if her partner was there, this wasn't going to be news she'd like.

CHAPTER TWENTY-ONE

"This better be good because I was in the middle of something." Kay slammed the door after they were both inside. "What the hell's going on?"

"We've got a clusterfuck of massive proportions," Paul said, turning to face her.

"Understatement of the year," Quinn said under his breath.

"Is somebody going to tell me what's happening?" She looked back and forth between them before Brenda standing in the kitchen doorway caught her attention. Paul turned to see what she was looking at and then held a hand up in a quick wave toward Brenda.

"Brenda Jansen is the woman you were telling me about?"

"Yes," Kay answered. Paul leaned closer to her and lowered his voice.

"Good. I always thought she deserved better than Janice." He straightened and walked toward Brenda. "I'll catch up with Brenda while Quinn fills you in on what's happening. He insisted on being the one to tell you anyway."

When Paul and Brenda disappeared back into the kitchen, Kay turned to see a perplexed look on Quinn's face.

"Who is she? You know Webber never agreed to let me be the one to tell you, so who is this woman who seems to have him eating out of the palm of her hand?"

"I'm hoping she's my girlfriend, but we can talk about it later." She led him into the living room and sat next to him on the couch. "Tell me what you came here to tell me about."

"Another woman was killed last night. The body was cleaned with bleach like the others, but she wasn't cut up and left in multiple locations. And this time he left a fingerprint on her belt buckle."

"Rayne?" Kay asked, at once feeling elated and horrified.

"We knew it was him before we even had the chance to run the print through the system because he left a note for us. He said he was coming after you next. He signed the note, and I think he probably left the fingerprint on purpose. He wants to be caught, but he wants you first. He was here in this housing development early this morning. A local cop pulled him over for a busted taillight but let him go." Quinn looked her in the eye and she knew she wasn't going to like what he said next. "I agree with Paul. You need to go somewhere safe until we can catch him, Griff. Besides, they want to put you on desk duty when you come back on Monday. The loo and the captain both think it would be a bad idea to have you out there where Rayne could take a free shot at you."

Kay sat in stunned silence. *Desk* duty? There was no way she'd stand for that, and Quinn knew it if the look on his face was any indication. She hadn't busted her ass all these years to be assigned to desk duty just because some lowlife had her in his sights. Kay felt amazingly calm when all she really wanted was to grab Rayne by the balls and twist them as hard as she could.

"Say something, Griff," Quinn said. "You scare the hell out of me when you're this quiet and you just got news I know pissed you off."

"I'm fine," she said. "You know I won't sit still for desk duty, so I guess I have no choice but to hide out until you guys catch him. I assume he's blowing in the wind now or else you'd have him in custody."

"Nobody's seen him since he was pulled over this morning. We've been to his apartment, his shop, his ex-wife's house, and even his sister's." Quinn was frustrated with the situation, and he wasn't doing anything to hide it from Kay. "It's only a matter of time until we catch him though."

"What have we decided?" Paul asked when he walked into the room, Brenda right beside him.

"Take me to a safe house," Kay said, never taking her eyes from Brenda's. Everything was so new with Brenda, but Kay knew without a doubt she would never do anything knowingly to put Brenda in danger. If disappearing for a week or two was the only way to protect her, she wouldn't fight it.

"I think Brenda may have come up with a viable solution." Paul glanced at Brenda, who nodded for him to continue. "Her parents have a vacation home on Lake Ontario in Canada. It's in her mother's maiden name so a cursory search won't tie either of you to it. The house is secluded enough there's only one road in. I think the place sounds perfect, and Rayne doesn't have a passport, so he won't be able to cross the border. At least not legally anyway."

Kay felt a lightness in her chest. That Brenda would do this for her meant more than she could say. It was a little overwhelming. Everything in the room faded away as she and Brenda looked at each other. Just when she thought she would have no choice but to carry Brenda upstairs to the bedroom, Quinn cleared his throat. Kay felt her cheeks flush at the knowing grin he gave her.

"When do I leave?" Kay managed to ask.

"I don't imagine my parents will have a problem with it, but I need to call and discuss it with them." Brenda looked unsure of herself, but Kay thought it made her look even sexier than she already was. "Then I would need to go home and pack a bag. Unless you wanted to go alone, of course."

"What could possibly make you think I wouldn't want you to go with me?"

"Quinn, come to the kitchen with me for a moment," Paul said. Kay was grateful for his good manners. She waited until they were gone before motioning for Brenda to take a seat on the couch beside her.

"I can't ask you to come with me, Brenda." Kay struggled not to look away from her intense gaze. "I hope you don't feel as though you have to."

"Hey, you gave me an out before and I didn't take it, remember?" Brenda took her hand and Kay nodded. "I'm not taking it now either. If you want to do this alone I would totally understand. But don't do it alone because you feel some need to protect me. Besides, you said we needed to talk after Paul left. Alone in a cottage on the lake for who knows how long will give us plenty of time to talk."

Kay could think of more pleasant things to do than talk, but she kept her ideas to herself. One of the things they needed to talk about was the possibility of her quitting the force. She'd thought about it a lot since the night she'd first mentioned it to Brenda. But Brenda's reaction when Paul called earlier was enough to convince Kay she needed to resign. Brenda had become more important to her than the job, and Kay wasn't about to prove her right by choosing it over her.

"I definitely want you to come with me. So call your parents and make sure everything's okay with them. Then go home and get your things so we can hurry the hell out of town. Maybe we can manage to convince ourselves we're taking a vacation."

Kay opened the door to Michael and Fran an hour later. Paul decided he didn't want her to be home alone in spite of the patrol cars parked in front and in the back of her house. He and Quinn had to get back to the business of finding Rayne, and she was glad for the company while she waited for Brenda to get back from her apartment.

"How are you holding up, sweetie?" Fran asked when they all settled in at the kitchen table.

Kay shrugged her response. Truth be told, she was fine. But she was worried about Brenda returning to her apartment by herself. Paul was right when he said they didn't have a reason to send someone with her, but knowing it didn't make it any easier to sit and wait. Kay had packed her things right after Brenda had left twenty minutes earlier.

"You want us to keep Max while you're gone?" Michael asked. Kay looked at him and shook her head. Mike was a big guy—a former college football player. She'd always felt safer when he was around.

"He's coming with us. I'd feel better knowing he's there to keep an eye on things while we're sleeping. He may be a pussycat when he knows you, but he's a hell of a watch dog." As if on cue, Max came trotting into the kitchen and sat next to her chair before resting his chin on her thigh. His soulful brown eyes seemed to beg her to scratch his ears, and she was powerless to resist his doggy charm.

"So when do I get to meet this woman who seems to have captured your heart?" Mike smiled, and she was appreciative of his knack for knowing when she didn't want to talk about something. Rayne had enough control over the situation as it was. She wasn't about to give him any more control by talking about him constantly.

"Probably in about an hour when she gets back here," Kay answered.

"Is she worthy of you?"

"Jesus, Mike," Fran said with a swat to his forearm. "Interfere much?"

"I've known her since grade school, baby, and I've always looked out for her. I'm not going to change now. She's like my little sister."

"Except for when you tried like hell to get her to date you in high school, right? You forget Kay and I are best friends. She told me all about it." Fran smiled as she spoke and Kay couldn't help but laugh when Mike's cheeks turned red.

"Thank you both for coming over and sitting with me. You both mean the world to me, and I hope you know it."

They talked about mundane things for the next hour but Kay was getting antsy waiting for Brenda to return. Part of her—the insecure part she rarely let anyone see—wondered briefly if Brenda might have changed her mind about going. No, she told herself. That wouldn't happen. There was something special between them, and Kay couldn't wait to see Brenda again so she could tell her exactly how she felt about her.

Chapter Twenty-two

When Brenda walked into her apartment, she tossed her keys on the coffee table and went to take a cold shower. The scene with Kay on the back deck before Paul Webber called had her worked up, and it was apparent they weren't going to get the chance to finish what they'd started anytime soon.

Her parents had been more than willing to allow her and Kay the use of their cottage for however long they needed it. Of course they were worried about her, and her mother was never one to keep her concerns to herself.

"Brenda, are you sure you want to be involved with a cop? You always said you'd never be with someone again who would have to drop everything and run out the door at a moment's notice," she said, the uneasiness evident in her voice.

"I know, Mom, but do you remember what Grandma always told me? Your heart chooses who you fall in love with, not your head. I think I might really be falling for her. I need to see this through, and we'll be doing a lot of talking while we're at the cottage."

"Like hell you will," she heard her father mutter. Brenda hadn't known he was on the extension, but it didn't surprise her. She chuckled at his comment.

"Gary," her mother admonished him.

"What? You know as well as I do they won't be spending their time talking."

"Okay, I need to go now," Brenda said, knowing this conversation would end with her being more embarrassed than she already was if she let it go any further. "I'll swing by and get the keys after I pack my bag. I should be there in about half an hour."

She sat down to call Dana as she ran her fingers through her still damp hair. She was dreading this conversation, but knew it was something she had to do if she was going to be gone indefinitely.

"To what do I owe this extreme oddity?" Dana asked sarcastically. "You've barely talked to me at all since you started hanging out with your new love muffin. And I sure as hell didn't expect to hear from you this weekend after the display you two put on last night in the bar."

Brenda smiled and leaned her head back against the couch.

"I'm going to be out of town for a while, Dana," she told her.

"What do you mean?"

"Exactly what I said," was her answer. Short and sweet. It sounded pretty self-explanatory to her. "Kay and I are going away, and I needed to tell you because you'll have to find someone to take my place in the band until we get back."

"Why the hell didn't you say something about this to me last night?" Dana asked, sounding more than a bit perturbed.

"I would have told you, but I didn't know last night." Brenda put her feet up on the coffee table. "We didn't decide until this morning."

"We?" Dana asked and laughed, but there was no mirth in the sound. "Jesus, Bren, you've known this woman what? Two weeks?"

"It's been a lot longer than that, and you know it," Brenda said defensively. She'd hoped Dana would react the same way her parents had and give her her full support. But she knew Dana the drama queen would blow everything out of proportion.

"You're no better than a man, do you realize that?" Dana asked indignantly. "I mean, you have mind-blowing sex with a woman, and you're willing to follow her anywhere. Think about what you're doing, Bren. I mean, *really* think about it. How well do you know her?"

"Seriously? You're the one who's been giving me such a hard time about *not* sleeping with her." Brenda almost laughed at the absurdity of Dana's reasoning.

"Exactly. So you finally jump in the sack with her once and now you're going to follow her around like a puppy. It's pathetic."

Brenda decided to ignore her snide comments. She knew Dana was half-joking, and the other half was jealousy because she was moving on, and Dana wasn't. She wanted to tell Dana the real reason they were leaving town, but Kay told her not to. "I think I might be falling for her."

"Fuck," was the reply. Only Dana could make the word sound like it had four syllables.

"When you find the one, you just know it in your heart," Brenda said.

"Jesus, how sappy can you possibly be?" Dana asked cynically. "When exactly did you become such a romantic fool?"

"You were constantly hounding me to get back out there," Brenda reminded her. Why was it your friends were only happy for you when you weren't contemplating commitment?

"Yeah, for a simple, uncomplicated romp in the hay," Dana said with a dramatic sigh. "How could I have known you were going to fall for the first pretty face that came along? Although I will admit it's a damn pretty face. And body, too. Jesus, I can't believe you're doing this, but you know what? I know better than to think anything I could possibly say would change your mind. I just hope things work out for you, and you don't regret this somewhere down the road."

"Thanks." Brenda smiled. "I love you, Dana. You're a great friend."

"Yeah, yeah, yeah, whatever," she said as she sighed into the receiver. "I love you too. So where are you going, and how long will you be gone?"

"I don't know." Brenda hated lying to her, but there was no way she could tell Dana the truth. The less people who knew where they were going the better. "We're just going to drive and see where we end up. We probably won't be gone for too long. A week. Maybe two. I really don't know for sure."

"Jesus, are you serious? I really can't believe you're doing this, Bren."

"You said that already," Brenda pointed out.

"Fuck you," she said, and laughed. It had always been Dana's standard response when she couldn't think of anything else to say. "When are you leaving? Can we get together for a drink before you go?"

"We're leaving this afternoon, so I'm afraid not." Brenda looked at her watch. It was noon. "In fact we're leaving as soon as I make it back to her place. Can you do me a favor and feed the fish while I'm gone? You have a key and you know where their food is."

"Only if you let me keep them when you get back."

"Done. Move them to your place while I'm gone if you want." There was a knock on the door. "I've got to go. Somebody's here."

"Maybe it's lover girl and she couldn't wait for you to get back," Dana said.

"Smart ass." She disconnected the call before Dana had a chance to respond. She frowned as she walked toward the door. A quick glance through the peephole revealed nothing. Whoever it was stood just out of her sight. "Who is it?"

"Postal Service, ma'am," was the reply. "I have a certified letter you need to sign for."

As she unlocked the door and pulled it open, she only had a split second to realize Tommy Rayne was standing in front of her before she was struck in the head and her entire world went completely black.

❖

Tommy hurried into the apartment and, after pulling her clear of the door, closed it, and locked it behind himself. He'd hit her hard. He was worried for a moment he might have killed her. When he knelt to check for a pulse, he found one. It was weak, but it was there. He smiled.

He'd followed her into the building so he would know which apartment was hers, and then he'd gone back out to his car to keep an eye on the back door for a few minutes. When he had been satisfied there wasn't too much traffic in and out that door, he made the decision to move in on her. He was tired of waiting. Tired of cooling his heels while he kept his distance from Griffith. For the past month, he'd been a model citizen, lulling the cops into complacency until he'd finally made his move the night before and got away from his tail.

He looked around the apartment for something to cover the wound on her head, but found nothing. He finally decided to take his baseball hat off his head and put it on hers. You could still see the blood, but it was a little better. He grabbed a towel from the bathroom and wiped away what he could from her face, but it was still seeping out of the gash on her head.

Tommy didn't care. He had to get the hell out of here, in case the bitch came along looking for her little girlfriend. It just wouldn't do if he were to get caught before he could put his plan into motion. He pulled the rope from his pocket and tied her hands together before lifting her up and carrying her out to his car. He was ecstatic his luck was holding, and absolutely no one was around to witness what he was doing.

Tommy considered momentarily about going back to her apartment and cleaning up, but he figured there was no point. They would all know soon enough he had her. He planned on seeing to it himself.

He drove as many back roads as he could to get out of town. Twenty minutes later, he pulled into the garage of an abandoned house in Camden, New Jersey. He pulled a cell phone out of his pocket and took a deep breath before punching in the number and hitting send.

❖

Michael and Fran were doing their best to keep Kay's mind off the fact almost three hours had gone by since Brenda left to pack her bag. She wished like hell she'd insisted on going with her, and then the squad car outside would have been with them. With Rayne in the wind, there was no telling what he might do. She jumped when the house phone on the table in front of her rang, but she picked it up and walked toward the living room as she answered the call.

"Hello," she said, hoping it was Brenda.

"Kay? This is Gary Jansen. Is Brenda there?"

"No, she isn't." Kay's heart felt like it stopped beating for a moment and everything in her vision began to swim. She had a sinking feeling something terrible had happened. Her eyes met Fran's and she knew Fran could see her panic. She looked away quickly.

"She was supposed to be here to get the keys for the cottage, but she hasn't shown up. I've tried calling her cell phone, but it just goes straight to voice mail."

Kay's cell phone began to ring and she glanced at the screen. "Gary, can I call you right back? My lieutenant is calling on the other line." He didn't sound happy but he agreed, and Kay answered Paul's call as she hung up with Brenda's father. "Griffith," she said brusquely.

"Kay, we have a situation here," Paul said, his voice terse. She felt her heart begin to speed up. His tone indicated to her there was something seriously wrong. "Please tell me Brenda's there with you."

"No, she's not," was her reply, but her voice sounded a thousand miles away to her own ears. *Dear God, please don't let anything have happened to Brenda.* "Paul, tell me what the hell is going on."

"I just had a phone call from our friend Rayne," Paul said. "He claims he has her."

Kay dropped the phone as she fell to her knees, and was only vaguely aware of the battery skittering off to the side. The only thought that kept running through her mind was she would kill the bastard if he hurt Brenda. She was dimly aware of Fran and Michael both trying to help her to her feet, but at the moment all she wanted was to curl up in a ball and disappear.

But she couldn't. Brenda needed her, and she had to pull herself together. Max was barking agitatedly, obviously sensing her distress.

She pushed Fran's hands away as she desperately worked to put the battery back into her phone and call Paul back. She ignored Mike and Fran who were frantically asking what happened.

"Please shut up!" she yelled. Kay started to apologize, but then Paul answered, and her attention was with him once again. "What the hell does he want? Is she alive?"

"He said she is," was the only thing he could offer. "He wouldn't let me talk to her, Kay. He could be anywhere. Quinn is on his way to pick you up and bring you in. We need to sit down and figure out some kind of game plan."

"I'll be outside waiting for him," Kay said before disconnecting. She looked at Fran and Mike and didn't know what to say. She knew if she tried to explain what had happened she'd end up losing control. She wanted desperately to save that reaction for when she was face-to-face with Rayne. "I'm so sorry I yelled at you guys. Rayne claims he has Brenda."

"What can we do?" Fran asked.

"Nothing. I'm going to the station as soon as Quinn gets here, but I'll call you later, when I know what's happening."

She grabbed the house phone and hit the button to call the last person who'd called her. Gary answered on the first ring.

"Kay?" he asked.

"Gary," was all she managed to get out before her throat constricted. Michael placed his hand on the back of her neck and she pulled herself together. "Gary, I think Brenda's been abducted."

There was an eerie silence coming from the other end of the line, and Kay had to look at the phone to make sure they hadn't been disconnected.

"Gary?"

"I'm here," he said, his voice sounding choked. "What happened?"

Kay filled him in on what little information she'd gotten and told them she was headed to the station. She tried to discourage him and his wife from driving down there, but of course he wasn't going to be dissuaded. She couldn't blame him though. She was just worried they were going to put all the blame for what happened on her. They hung up and Kay gathered her things to head outside and wait for Quinn.

"Anything you need, Kay. Just let us know." Mike looked ready to beat someone up if she needed him to, and she loved him for it.

Kay hugged them both and promised to keep them updated as she pushed them out the door, following close behind. She looked at the sky and said a silent prayer to the God her parents were convinced hated her. As she pulled out her cell phone again to try to call Brenda, she heard tires squealing around the corner. She ran out to the street to jump into Quinn's car.

She swore to herself if anything happened to Brenda she'd kill Rayne herself.

Rayne smiled when he heard the cell phone ring. For about the twentieth time. But he was convinced this time—the first time it had rang since he'd called the police—it would be her. He'd ignored the other calls, but this one he would take.

The little dyke made noises like she was waking up, but when he grabbed her shoulder to force her onto her back, she passed out again. He found the phone in her jeans pocket and pulled it out. The smart thing would have been to get rid of the SIM card and toss the phone, but he wanted this. He *wanted* Griffith to know what he'd done, and for her to hear the words from his own mouth.

"I was wondering how long it would take you to call, Detective," Rayne said into the phone. He was going to enjoy this.

"What the hell do you want?" Griffith asked.

She sounded calm, but Rayne knew better. She was controlling her emotions so as not to give him the upper hand. Rayne laughed, but then quickly turned serious.

"I want you," he said, his voice low and menacing. "I'll exchange her for you, and that is the only deal I'll make with any of you people."

"I want to talk to her. I need to know she's still alive before we discuss any kind of deal, Tommy."

"Later," Rayne answered. He glanced down at the woman lying on the floor and smiled. "She's a little tied up at the moment, and she's lost a lot of blood. I probably shouldn't have hit her as hard as I did with that crowbar. I'll call you at this number tonight at eight o'clock. Maybe I'll let you talk to your dyke lover then, Detective."

Tommy put the phone in his pocket and sat back to contemplate what his next move would be. Griffith's girlfriend was more attractive up close and personal if you ignored the blood all over her face. He was itching to kill again, but he knew this one was worth more to him alive. If she was dead, he'd never get Griffith. As long as this one was alive, he was in control. He smiled before he pushed her with his foot. She groaned and curled up in the fetal position as he made his way back outside.

CHAPTER TWENTY-THREE

Quinn called Paul when they entered the parking garage and told him they were on their way up. When the elevator doors opened, Paul was there waiting for them. He motioned for Quinn to go on into the squad room and held Kay back.

"Her parents are in my office," he said before leading her there.

He didn't sound happy. No doubt they were raising hell for them allowing this to happen to Brenda. When they walked past Quinn at his desk he mouthed *what?* She shrugged but kept on walking. She wasn't looking forward to this conversation.

"Is there any news?" Laura asked the second Kay was in Paul's office. She'd been crying, which was obvious by the red eyes and the tissue she held in her hand.

"I talked to Rayne on the way here." Kay waited until everyone was seated before relaying to them the details of the conversation. She left out the part about Brenda having lost a lot of blood. There was no reason for her parents to hear that. She felt as though she were on autopilot. Her emotions kept threatening to rise to the surface, but so far she was successful in tamping them down.

"So what now?" Gary asked.

"We wait for him to call Kay tonight as he instructed," Paul answered. When Gary looked like he was about to burst a blood vessel, Paul put a hand up. "I assure you we have all available personnel out there looking for her, Mr. and Mrs. Jansen. But if we can't find him, our only choice is to wait and see what his demands are."

Kay looked at her hands folded in her lap. She'd left out the part of the conversation where Rayne demanded her for Brenda. She'd tell Paul later, but again, the Jansens didn't need to know it. So far they hadn't blamed her, but that information might be all they needed to tip them over the edge.

"You'll keep us updated?" Laura asked through her tears.

"Constantly," Paul assured them. "As soon as we learn anything, either Kay or I will call you. I don't mean to sound callous, but there's nothing for you to do at this point other than to wait and let us do our jobs."

"Please just bring her home safely," Gary said.

"Trust me when I say that's my objective, sir," Kay said. "I will do everything in my power to make sure it happens."

Paul asked her to wait for him in his office as he walked the Jansens to the elevator. She spent the time standing at the window looking out at the squad room. When he returned, he waited for her to sit again before speaking.

"There's no way I'm going to convince you to go home and wait, is there?"

"If you thought there was any chance of that you never would have sent Quinn to pick me up and bring me in." Kay held his gaze and he finally looked away with a nod. She watched as he opened the top drawer of his desk. She was surprised when he pulled out her weapon and badge. He set them on the desk, but she made no move to reach for them.

"You're back as of now, Griffith. I'm not sure I'd let you go home and wait it out anyway. Rayne's beef is with you now, and you'd be a sitting duck. At least this way I can keep an eye on you."

"Is the captain okay with this?" she asked. The last thing she wanted was for Paul to get in trouble because of her.

"He's on vacation this week, so I'm making the decision to put you on full duty." Paul ran a hand over his bald head. "Just don't do anything to make me regret this, Kay."

She nodded and got to her feet. She picked up her weapon and badge before hugging him quickly. "Thank you, Paul. All I want is to get Brenda away from this fucker."

"That's what we all want," he said. Just as she was about to walk out the door he said. "Oh, and, Kay? You're taking lead on this case."

"All right, people, I need you to listen up," Paul said to the homicide department as they sat around a table in the conference room. "We have less than five hours before Griffith makes contact with the suspect again. We need to try and figure out what we're going to do."

"Why is she even here?" a voice from the other end of the table asked. Kay recognized John Porter's somewhat nasally monotone, and closed her eyes momentarily. There were few people in the world she truly despised, but John Porter was definitely one of them. "She's still out on suspension, isn't she?"

"She's been cleared to return," Paul replied, his tone clipped. She hoped again he wouldn't get into too much trouble with the brass for letting her join in on the investigation. If Colley or Porter found out he'd made the decision on his own, they'd be the first ones to cause waves over it. "Rayne's problem is with her because of what happened between the two of them, and he's refusing to deal with anyone but her. If she wasn't here with us as her backup, he would have dragged her into it alone, and personally, I feel better with her here. Griffith is taking the lead on this case, so nobody moves without her okay."

"What the fuck?" Dale Colley muttered. Kay smiled to herself. There was someone else she hated. Porter and Colley were unquestionably old school and didn't think women belonged *anywhere* in the police force. Barefoot and pregnant was the way they liked their women, and Kay was shocked they were both married. What kind of woman would want to be with a man so bigoted? At least Paul had enough sense to not partner them together. Their attitudes would get them into a hell of a lot of trouble if they were out on the streets in the same vehicle.

"Rayne only wants to deal with her," Paul repeated. "If he wants to deal with her, then that's what he's going to get. Does anyone have a problem with that?"

No one did. At least not anyone who was willing to speak up. Kay was fairly certain Porter and Colley were the only ones who would object to her heading up the investigation anyway.

"Why the hell are we wasting our time trying to save a fucking dyke?" a whispered comment from the other side of the room came. It sounded to Kay like it had been Colley again. She was about to stand up, but Paul put a hand firmly on her shoulder to keep her in her chair as he shook his head. Maybe this was what he'd meant when he'd said not to make him regret bringing her in. She bit her tongue to keep from verbally assaulting the prick.

"Porter, Colley, I want you two the hell out of here," he said, somehow managing to stay calm. Kay knew he was almost as worried about Brenda as she was. It was always harder when the victim was someone you knew personally. "You're both off this case, as of now. I don't need your prejudiced way of thinking hindering what progress we might make."

They both sat there in stunned silence for a moment before Colley laughed and stood up.

"You people are pathetic," he said, but his attention was fixed on Kay. She refused to look at him. "Women don't belong in this job, and now you're going to take orders from one?"

No one spoke as Porter stood up too and they both stormed out of the room. Once they were gone, all eyes went back to the lieutenant, and Kay thought she heard a collective sigh of relief from the men who still remained. It seemed there weren't many John Porter and Dale Colley fans in the room. She wondered briefly if sensitivity training would help them, but since the class was probably run by a woman, she highly doubted it.

"What did he say to you?" Paul asked Kay, speaking about Rayne. He took a seat at the head of the table.

"He said she was tied up and had lost a lot of blood," Kay said quietly, knowing she was only relaying the information for the other detectives' benefit. Paul already knew some of the details. She avoided looking at any of her colleagues because she knew she'd lose it and start crying. She was doing her best to try to stay detached from the situation, but it wasn't working. She took a deep breath because she knew Paul would never go for what she was going to say next. She looked at him pointedly. "He wants to make an exchange. Me for her."

"Out of the question," Paul replied, shaking his head vehemently.

"Not as far as I'm concerned," Kay said. She had to save Brenda, even if it meant giving herself to this scum. Brenda hadn't asked for any of this, and at the moment she would do *anything* to ensure Brenda's safety. "If we can set up an exchange, we can have snipers there waiting for him."

"If it comes to that, we'll discuss it then," Paul said. It was as much of an okay as he would ever give. Kay quickly decided she'd have to take it—at least for now. Paul glanced over at Quinn. "Have we found anything in his apartment that might indicate where he could have taken her?"

"We've gone over it twice." Quinn shook his head in obvious frustration. "We've been through his sister's house too, but she claims she hasn't spoken to him in over a year. Same thing with the ex-wife."

"Somebody married him?" Ryan Elam asked. There were a couple of chuckles from around the room.

"Somebody married Porter and Colley too," Quinn answered. "There really must be someone for everyone."

"Enough," Paul said with pointed stares at both Quinn and Elam. "What about Brenda's apartment?"

"Nothing," Jack Becker spoke up from the other side of the table. Kay looked over at him as he winced and then turned away from her. "Just a lot of blood, and forensics is checking on it as we speak."

"What about the pawnshop?" Kay asked, trying not to think about Brenda being hurt. Quinn again shook his head. "Then I'm going back over there. Even if there's nothing there, I might be able to get some information from the owner of the bar next door."

"The gay bar?" Elam asked with a chuckle. Kay watched as Becker slugged Elam in the arm and Elam stood up to tower over him. "What the fuck is your problem, dude?"

"You're my problem at the moment," Becker answered. Jack had come to homicide a year after Kay, and the two of them had always had a decent working relationship. He'd never had a problem with her being a woman—unlike the two detectives that had already been unceremoniously thrown out of the room.

"You been hanging out with the gays, Jack?" Elam asked. "You and Griff got something to tell the rest of us?"

Kay glanced over at Paul, who only shrugged. She'd always kept her private life private, and had never come out to anyone other than Paul and Quinn. Kay was sure the other detectives suspected she was gay, but no one had ever asked, so she never told. Paul's shrug was his way of letting her know it was up to her if she wanted to open up to the rest of the squad. What did she care if they talked behind her back now? She motioned for Paul to step out of the room with her.

"What's wrong?" he asked with deep concern as the door closed behind them. His hand was resting gently on the small of her back.

"I never should have let Brenda go home alone, Paul." Kay fought the tears that threatened. She wasn't sure how much longer she could hold it in. "If she's already dead, I swear I'll kill him myself."

"Kay, we have to move ahead with this investigation believing she's still alive. If you go forward thinking otherwise, you'll be no good to me. Do you understand?"

"When this is over, will I be put back on desk duty?"

"I can't say for sure what's going to happen. I'm not even sure I'll survive the shit storm that'll come for allowing you to take lead on this when you aren't officially cleared for full duty yet."

"Then I'll make it easier on you," Kay said. She took a deep breath and went on before she could talk herself out of it. "When this is done, you'll have my badge and weapon back. I can't do this job anymore."

"Don't make any rash decisions, Kay. We'll talk about this later."

"I've had almost eight weeks to think about it, Paul. I'm not going to change my mind. If we rescue Brenda, there's no way in hell I'll risk this happening to her again. If we don't..." Kay looked away and closed her eyes. She didn't want to think of the possibility Brenda might not make it out of this alive. "I wouldn't be able to do my job effectively if we don't."

"Kay—"

"There's no room for discussion on this, Paul, and I'm going to tell the rest of the squad." She jerked a thumb over her shoulder toward the other detectives seated in the conference room. She was still trying to shove her emotions aside and force herself to look at the situation as a detective and not as a woman whose lover had been abducted by a sadistic killer. "I only wanted to bring you out here to let you know first. I didn't want to catch you off guard with it, and I figured you deserved a heads up."

"Kay, think about what you're saying here," he pleaded. "Do you really want to throw away your career?"

"I already have," she said, forcing a smile. She placed a hand on his arm. "I did that the second I slammed the butt of my gun into Rayne's nose. You know it as well as I do. I need to get out of here, or I'll end up going crazy."

He nodded slowly, obviously resigned to the fact she had her mind made up. Or maybe he decided not to argue because he thought they could discuss the future later. Kay had made her decision though, and she knew he wouldn't be able to talk her out of it, no matter how hard he tried. He hugged her briefly before they walked back into the room. Kay stood at the head of the table as she took a deep breath, and Paul took her seat as the rest of the detectives waited for her to say whatever it was she was going to say.

"Ryan, what was your question before I left the room?" she asked, knowing full well what it had been, but wanting him to repeat it for the benefit of the others who may not have been paying attention. She wanted to be sure everyone understood what she was about to tell them. He glanced around nervously.

"I asked if you and Becker had something you needed to tell us," he said. Kay took another deep breath before answering.

"Well, I can't speak for Jack, but I'm sure his wife and three kids could. But as for myself, yes, I'm a lesbian," she said after a moment. Her heart was pounding. She'd never thought she would be coming out to the entire department at once. "Brenda Jansen, the woman who Rayne has captive, is my girlfriend. Given the fact this scumbag has it out for me, I'd be willing to bet the *only* reason he has her is because she's my girlfriend. I can't even think of any other reason she'd be on his radar. Now, I'd like to think we can all be professional about this. Once the case is over, I'll be resigning my position. I'm moving on with my life. My number one priority is getting her away from him—alive."

Everyone seemed stunned, except for Paul and Quinn. Quinn had never been one to let his emotions show. If he was surprised by her announcement to resign, he kept it under wraps. Kay knew she'd hear about it later.

"Is this going to be a problem for anyone here?" Paul asked gruffly, but it was both he and Quinn who turned to look at the other detectives. Kay found herself smiling at her two self-proclaimed protectors. Everyone in the room just shook their heads.

"I have a problem with it," Becker said after a moment. Kay felt her heart sink. He stood and cleared his throat. "I don't want you to resign. You're a damn good detective, Kay. It just wouldn't be the same around here without you."

Kay went to him and hugged him as she wiped a tear from her cheek.

"Thank you," she said, a bit choked up.

"We'll do everything we can to get her away from him, Kay," Ryan Elam assured her.

"Then let's find this bastard," Paul said. "The sooner the better."

CHAPTER TWENTY-FOUR

"Excuse me," Kay said to Carol as she and Quinn walked into the building. She hadn't been introduced to the bar's owner the night before, but Brenda had told Kay her name. It was only two in the afternoon and the bar was obviously closed, but they followed a deliveryman in the front door.

"We aren't open," she said in the tone of voice that told Kay she had to tell a lot of people the same thing. It took a moment for her to turn and face them.

"I'm Kay Griffith and this is my partner, Larry Quinn." Kay pulled out her badge and flashed it for her to see. She seemed to be a little bit surprised as she looked back and forth from Kay to Quinn.

"I apologize for the rude greeting. I'm Carol, owner and head bartender of Discovery. What can I do for you?" she asked.

Kay hesitated and wondered how to even broach the subject. She glanced at Quinn, who was wandering around the place and obviously not going to help her out. She cleared her throat and turned her attention back to Carol.

"I've been dating Brenda, the drummer in the band you had playing here last night." Kay took a seat at the bar. "What do you know about Tommy Rayne?"

"Other than the fact he's a scumbag?" she answered, offering a soda, which Kay accepted. "What else is there to know?"

"Have you seen him at all in the past twenty-four hours?"

"No, I haven't seen him since last weekend, but that doesn't mean anything. He's almost always at his shop, and I don't make it a point of looking for him," she answered with a shake of her head. She met Kay's eyes and Kay had the feeling she was being evaluated. Even if Brenda had never mentioned her, it was obvious Carol was a friend. "Does Brenda know you're a cop? She told me she was seeing someone, but she never said it was a cop."

"Would you happen to know where Rayne might be?" Quinn interrupted as he took a seat next to Kay at the bar.

"I talk to him as little as possible," she assured them both. "Is this about those two murders a while back? Wait a minute. I know you. You're the one who broke his nose, aren't you?"

"Yes, I am," Kay said.

"Good for you, honey. God knows I've wanted to haul off and hit him more than once." Carol swiped a towel over a nonexistent spill on the bar. Kay realized Carol was older than she'd first thought. The crow's feet around her eyes and the gray hair put her somewhere in her fifties as near as she could tell. "He comes in here once in a while for a drink, but I've told him not to come back. The girls here are more than a little creeped out by him."

"Griff, you're a legend," Quinn joked with an elbow to her ribs.

"Fuck you," Kay muttered before turning back to Carol. "In order to get back at me for assaulting him, Rayne's abducted Brenda. If you can tell us anything—anything at all—we would greatly appreciate it."

"He has Brenda?" she asked in disbelief, and Kay nodded.

"We need to find him, Carol," Kay said, completely understanding her shock, but not having the luxury of letting the numbness take hold. Kay thought she herself would probably welcome the lack of feeling that accompanied shock. At the moment though, she didn't have the time to console—or to be consoled. "I'm not sure how much time we have."

"I know there have been times he's stayed at his store all night," Carol said with a shrug. "At least, his car was behind the building overnight."

"And you're sure you haven't seen him today?" Quinn asked.

"I've only been here about an hour or so. I haven't seen him at all."

"Please, will you give us a call if you do see him, or if anything unusual happens?" Kay asked as she took a card out of her back pocket and handed it to her. "Here's my cell phone number. Would you mind if we go out the back door? We'd like to take a look around."

"Be my guest." Carol nodded and showed them the way.

Kay nodded her thanks as she and Quinn headed to the back. It was a small parking lot, as the majority of the customers parked on the street out front. Mostly employees used this lot, and currently Carol's sedan and a car that was not Tommy's Honda Civic were the only vehicles present.

"Why didn't you tell me you were going to resign, Kay?" Quinn asked. It was the first time he'd mentioned it, and even though he tried not to, he sounded hurt.

"Paul didn't even know until I pulled him out of the conference room this afternoon," she assured him. "I don't think I seriously made up my mind until you told me I'd be on desk duty when I came back. But I've been thinking about it for longer than I care to think about."

"Kay, come take a look," Quinn said urgently. She'd begun walking in the opposite direction, and turned to see him kneeling by the Dumpster. She strode quickly over to kneel next to him. She saw he was pointing at a small puddle of what appeared to be blood as he looked over at her.

"Call forensics—and, Paul," Kay said, trying to keep the anxiety out of her voice. She refused to fall apart now. There would be plenty of time for that after Brenda was safe. Kay glanced up at the open Dumpster, dreading what she might find inside it. There was a part of her that reasoned it wouldn't be Brenda. Rayne would keep her alive for now, at least until he could get his hands on Kay. She peered into the Dumpster, but there was too much trash in it. She would have to climb in. "I want to know if it's hers, and I want to know ASAP. They can compare it to the blood in her apartment."

"I'll make sure there's a rush on it," he said.

Quinn walked a few feet away to make his calls as Kay pulled herself up and over, landing inside the Dumpster. She thought vaguely she could be contaminating the scene, but she had to know if Brenda's body had been dumped. Thankfully, it didn't take long to discover there was not a body inside the Dumpster. As she pulled herself back out, she looked over toward the back door of Rayne's pawnshop.

"They're on their way," Quinn said as he put his phone away.

"We're going back in there," Kay said with unwavering determination. She headed for the door with Quinn right on her heels. She knew he wasn't about to let her go in there alone.

The door was locked from the inside, so they ended up having to go in through the front door, and Kay pulled her gun as soon as they were inside. They'd gone through here before having their talk with Carol and had found nothing. The basement was filled with a lot of crap, but there was no sign of Rayne—or Brenda—anywhere in the building. They didn't find anything different the second time through.

Billy was working again, and he'd been anything but helpful, but he had at least allowed them to look around. He didn't seem any less nervous than he'd been the day Kay broke Rayne's nose. She wondered if he was always this way, or if it was only when there were cops around. He obviously didn't know enough to demand they show him a search warrant before allowing them entry, but Kay was beyond following procedure anyway. What could they do—suspend her again? If the situation wasn't so dire, she might have laughed at the thought.

She gave Billy her cell phone number and urged him to call if Rayne showed up, or if anything out of the ordinary happened. He assured her he would as he shoved the card into his back pocket, though Kay had no doubt it would end up in the trash as soon as they walked out the door.

They hung around out back to wait for the forensics team to show up before heading back into the station.

CHAPTER TWENTY-FIVE

When Brenda finally woke up, it didn't take her long to realize her hands were tied together, as were her ankles. There was tape over her mouth that was making it much more difficult to breathe. She opened her eyes, but it didn't make a difference, as everything surrounding her was still pitch-black. She panicked for a moment but concentrated on steadying her breathing in order to calm herself.

There was faint music coming from somewhere, but she couldn't tell where, or even what kind of music it was. There was water dripping off to her right. Her first thought was she must be in the basement of her apartment building. It was an area off limits to tenants and was underneath the laundry room and storage area. Rayne wouldn't have wanted to risk carrying her out of the building in broad daylight, would he?

Then again, she had no idea how long she'd been out. For all she knew, days had passed since he'd abducted her. The pain in her head was excruciating. She fought to keep her eyes open since her vision was slowly adjusting to the darkness.

She began to notice a stench in the room. She'd never smelled a dead body before, but when she was about ten, they'd discovered a dead raccoon in the basement that smelled similar to this. Except for the faint smell of bleach along with it.

Dear God, please let it be a dead animal.

She tried desperately to think of something more pleasant and not of the stories she'd heard on the news and read in the paper. The stories about how the bodies were cleaned of all evidence using some type of bleach mixture before they were hacked into pieces, and how their hearts had been cut out of their chests.

It was futile to try to free her hands. That much she had figured out within moments of regaining consciousness. It seemed as though every time she tried, the rope only got tighter around her wrists.

He had her lying on her right side, and her shoulder was killing her. The concrete floor beneath her was brutal. She vaguely remembered her cell phone ringing at some time, and he had pushed her over on her back to remove it from her pocket.

As she tried in vain to lift her head, she realized there was something wet and sticky under it, and she could only assume it was her own blood since the metallic taste in her mouth was so overpowering. She had a memory of Rayne hitting her in the head with something—a gun? A crowbar? She didn't know, and it was hurting her head even more trying to remember.

In the darkness, she noticed a dim light coming from somewhere. She tried to squint in order to see it more clearly. The overhead lights came on, and to her amazement, music was piped into the room, successfully drowning out the faint music she'd heard when she first regained consciousness.

It was very soothing music being channeled in, and it surprised her Tommy Rayne would choose classical music. She would have thought he'd be more of a heavy metal or grunge rock fan. Brenda had to close her eyes against the unexpected brightness of the lights. After a moment, she heard a door and forced her eyes open so she could look in the direction the noise had come from, but all she could make out was a rickety staircase leading up.

"Glad to see you're finally awake," Rayne said as he picked up a chair and brought it over to her. He picked her up roughly by grabbing her under the arms and sat her down hard in the chair before going and getting another one for himself, which he put so it was facing her. "We'll be calling your girlfriend in a minute."

Kay.

She knew Kay would be doing everything in her power to find her, but Brenda hoped to God she wasn't doing it alone. How the hell would they ever find her? Brenda just looked at him, trying her best to focus her eyes, and not wanting him to know how much pain she was in. She was pretty sure her right shoulder was dislocated, and she could feel blood seeping down the side of her face. She fought valiantly to keep her head up straight, even though it wanted desperately to fall forward.

He laughed as he reached across the space between them. Brenda braced herself for the pain she knew would follow when he grabbed a corner of the tape covering her mouth. Rayne ripped it off without hesitation, and she forced her eyes to stay open through the pain. She glanced around the room, afraid she would see a dead body lying around, but she was unable to keep herself from looking. There was nothing.

The room was completely empty except for the two chairs and the speakers on the ceiling in each corner. Brenda did notice a big section of the floor that hadn't been finished with concrete. Or perhaps it had been torn up. It was merely dirt, and in one part, there was an obvious mound, as if someone had been digging.

She was careful not to let her eyes linger in any one place for too long, and turned her attention back to Rayne. It wasn't like she could focus enough on any one place for too long anyway. Which was a good thing, because if she could focus, she knew it would be his missing eye her attention was drawn to. She had a feeling staring at it would only succeed in pissing him off, and she definitely didn't want to do that.

"She's going to want to talk to you," he said. There was nothing but hatred in his eye and in his voice. She could see it as plain as day, even with the lack of focus.

"What do you want from me?" she asked, her throat terribly dry.

"I don't want anything from *you*," he said with a high-pitched maniacal laugh. If she closed her eyes she could picture the Joker from *Batman* when he laughed. He turned serious, and the quick change startled Brenda. His voice was low and menacing. "I want *her*. She's gonna pay for what she did to me."

"Kay won't give you shit," she said, almost spitting the words at him. So much for not pissing him off. He surprised her though by staying calm.

"Oh, yes she will—if she ever wants to see you alive again," he said. He reached over and grabbed her by the chin, forcing her head one way, and then the other. "You're a feisty one, aren't you? I was afraid I'd killed you when I hit you on the head."

Brenda just stared into his eye, forcing herself to not look at the empty socket. She was determined not to give him any satisfaction at all. She was in more pain than she'd ever been in before in her life, but she tried to block it out of her mind by focusing on Kay's image. What popped into her mind was the vision of Kay answering the door the first morning in her bikini. It caused Brenda to smile.

That was her mistake.

Rayne obviously thought she was mocking him. He stood and backhanded her hard across the cheek. Brenda fell sideways off the chair, crying out when she landed on her shoulder. He forcefully picked her up again and threw her back into the chair. When the chair started to tip backward, he grabbed her by the front of her T-shirt and steadied her.

"You think you're smarter than me, you fucking dyke?" he asked angrily, not letting go of her shirt. He leaned toward her and looked as if he was going to hit her again, but she didn't flinch. Not even when his spittle landed on her face. He smiled and nodded his head as he let go of her. Brenda continued to stare at him as he scratched his back with both hands, up high, between the shoulder blades. She'd seen him do it before, and always wondered what the hell he was doing. She decided now was not the time to make fun of him by asking. After a moment, he resumed his seat and removed a cell phone from his pocket. It wasn't hers though. He must have gotten rid of it so they couldn't use the cell towers to find them.

He dialed a number and sat back as he raised it to his ear and waited, smiling.

"I want to talk to her, Tommy," Kay said. She was talking loud enough for Brenda to hear her clearly. "If you can't prove to me she's all right, there will be no chance of a deal."

"You're in luck, detective," he said with a surprising amount of respect. Brenda could see he was only fucking with Kay though, and it pissed her off. "She's right here."

He held the phone to Brenda's ear, but pulled the bottom of his shirt up to reveal the butt of a 9 mm. He saw Brenda glance at it, and then he nodded for her to talk.

"Kay?" she said, her voice shaking.

"Oh, God, Brenda," Kay said, and she began to cry. "Are you hurt badly?"

"No," she lied, finally able to focus in on Rayne's eye for a moment. What good would it do to upset Kay further? Brenda was pretty sure her injuries weren't life threatening. If they were, she probably wouldn't still be alive. She took a deep breath, hating herself for not being brave enough to have said the words in person. "I love you, Kay."

"Enough," Rayne said as he pulled the phone away from her. He put it back to his own ear, and sat back in his chair. "Are you satisfied, bitch?"

"No," Kay said. "I wasn't done talking to her, Tommy. Put her back on."

"I don't think so," he replied, and he smiled as he began to pace back and forth. He glanced at his watch. "I'll call you tomorrow evening, five sharp. And be ready to talk about a deal. *Maybe* I'll let you talk to her again then."

The line went dead in Kay's ear, and she slammed the phone down on her desk. She put her head down on her arms and cried quietly. She hadn't realized until she heard Brenda's voice how much she'd been hoping this was all a bad dream. But she was alive. Kay had to hold on to that fact. Aside from the shakiness in her voice, she sounded strong.

"Kay," Paul said as he gently put a hand on her shoulder. "Did he make any demands?"

She lifted her head and wiped her eyes as she shook her head. They had tech people recording the call, but she knew Paul wouldn't know yet what had been said from Rayne's end. Paul sat next to her and waved the rest of the detectives away, except for Quinn, whose desk pushed up to face hers.

"He's going to call again tomorrow with his demands," she told them quietly.

"She's all right though, right?" Quinn asked.

"She's alive." Kay shrugged and sat back in her seat. "She said she isn't badly hurt, but I don't believe her given how much blood Elam said was at the scene. I think she just doesn't want to worry me."

"Listen to me, Kay," Paul said. "I've called Fran to come and pick you up tonight. I need you to get some sleep. Otherwise you'll be no good to us tomorrow. There's nothing else you can do for her tonight anyway, and Brenda needs you to be at your best. You've already been going nonstop for more than nine hours now. I'll have the SWAT team ready to deploy as soon as he tells us when and where he wants to make the exchange"

"I can pick you up tomorrow if you want," Quinn offered. Kay managed a weak smile in his direction.

"I can't go home, Paul," she said, shaking her head. "I need to be here."

"Why?" he asked. "You won't talk to him again until tomorrow evening. There's no reason for you to stay. Go with Fran, get something to eat, and get some sleep. Maybe a new perspective tomorrow will help us."

She began to protest some more, but she saw Paul wave in the direction of the elevators. Kay looked, and Fran was hurrying in their direction. There was no point in arguing when there were three of them against her. Four, if she counted Michael, and she knew he would be on their side. She knew enough to back down, and besides, Paul was right.

Kay hugged Fran tightly, not able to stop the crying when it started again, and Fran did her best to comfort her.

"Come on, honey, I'll take you home," she said soothingly, and then helped her to get her things together.

"Do you need me to pick you up tomorrow?" Quinn asked as he stood also. Kay shook her head.

"I can drive myself, but thank you," she said before hugging first him, and then Paul. "Thank you both. I'll see you tomorrow."

"Make sure she eats something and gets some sleep," Paul told Fran as they were walking away. She nodded and waved at him.

Tommy shut the phone off again as soon as he was done talking to the bitch. It was a burner he'd bought at the local Walmart, and he had a few others too. He needed to get rid of this one far enough away from here that they wouldn't be able to pinpoint his location. He thought about just tying Brenda up and making her spend the night sitting in the chair, but in the end he decided to lay her back down on the ground. She had passed out on him again, and it was a little alarming that the gash in her head was still seeping blood. This would all be for nothing if the little dyke were to die on him.

He flexed the hand he'd used to hit her earlier. It had hurt like hell, and he knew he probably shouldn't have done it, but she'd been laughing at him, goddamn it. If there was one thing he couldn't stand, it was people laughing at him.

After considering briefly whether or not to try to clean up her wound, he eventually decided against it. What did it matter if the little dyke died? It would still succeed in hurting the bitch, and maybe it would be even better than actually killing Griffith.

He smiled at the thought of hurting her. He knew one way or the other this would all be over soon. He just hoped he got his chance at Griffith before they succeeded in taking him down for good.

❖

Brenda allowed her eyes to open only after she heard the door close, and a few seconds later, the lights and the piped in classical music went off, allowing the other faint music to drift back down to her. She thought she recognized it, but couldn't concentrate long enough to be completely sure. It sounded like her band. It almost sounded like Dana singing. Was it possible she was underneath the bar?

She looked around her, but it was so dark she couldn't make anything out. She wasn't even sure there *was* a basement under the bar. Carol kept her liquor supply in a huge storage room behind the bar.

But where else could she possibly be that Dana and the band would be practicing? She had to be there. She had to think of some way to relay this information to Kay, if this bastard ever allowed her to talk to Kay again.

She closed her eyes and tried desperately to think of Kay. When this was over and Rayne was either dead or in jail, she intended to still take Kay away for a week or two to the cottage in Canada. She held on to the thought as she drifted into an exhausted sleep.

CHAPTER TWENTY-SIX

"Kay, won't you please talk to me?" Fran begged after riding most of the way in an uncomfortable silence.

She was just making the turn into Kay's development, and they hadn't said more than a few sentences to each other until now. Kay had spent the better part of the ride trying unsuccessfully on her cell phone to get in touch with Gary and Laura Jansen. Obviously, the only positive thing she had to tell them was she'd spoken with Brenda, and she finally left a message saying as much to them. At least they all knew she was still alive.

"I should try and get in touch with Dana," was all Kay could manage to say.

"Dana?" Fran asked. "Isn't she the singer?"

"And Brenda's best friend," Kay answered, but she realized she didn't have Dana's phone number. She didn't know Dana's last name, or even where she worked. How the hell could she get in touch with her? The only thing Kay could think was if she were in Dana's shoes, she would want to know what was going on.

"Maybe you should call her," Fran suggested as Kay began to cry again.

"I can't," was all she said.

"Then I'll call her," Fran offered. "You can give me the number when we get to your house, all right? I'll do it for you, honey."

"No, I mean I can't. I don't know her number," Kay said, trying her best to dry her eyes. They turned onto her street, and she saw the lights were on in her house. What the hell was going on? Had she left them on that morning when she'd left with Quinn? "Did we leave the lights on when you and Michael were here this morning?"

"No, it was daylight. I'm pretty sure there weren't any lights on," Fran said, pulling into the driveway and shutting the car off. "Maybe Michael came over here and turned them on when I left to pick you up. You know, so we wouldn't be walking into a dark house."

"Call him and find out." Kay pulled her weapon from her shoulder holster and checked to make sure it was loaded before opening her door.

"Kay—"

"Call him," Kay said, her voice cold. She watched the windows for any movement but saw nothing. She hoped to God Rayne was in the house. She'd love nothing more than to put an end to this shit tonight. Maybe then she and Brenda could move on with their lives.

She went slowly up the walk to the front door, her gun poised to shoot. Kay breathed through her nose, trying to calm herself. To center herself. She'd never had to use her weapon before, but she'd show no mercy to Rayne.

"Kay!" Fran yelled in a hushed voice just before Kay reached the door. Kay looked over her shoulder to see her still by the car, waving for Kay to come back. Kay took a deep breath before heading back to her. "Michael says he wasn't here. Do you think it's Rayne?"

"Who else could it be? You're the only one who has a key to the house." Kay holstered her weapon and pulled her cell phone from her pocket. She called Paul and told him what was happening. He told her to stay put and they'd be there in a few minutes.

"It's all clear," Quinn said as he and Ryan Elam emerged from the house forty-five minutes later. He handed a cell phone and a piece of paper, both enclosed in plastic evidence bags, to Paul.

"What's that?" Kay asked, recognizing the phone as Brenda's. Paul read the note before handing both bags to her. She turned the phone on and her breath caught when she saw the picture that came up. It was Brenda, obviously unconscious. She was lying on a concrete floor, a pool of blood around her head.

"I already checked the details of the picture," Quinn said before she could even think to form the question in her mind. "It was taken early this afternoon, before you talked to her tonight. She's alive, Griff. Hold on to that."

She handed the phone to Fran before turning her attention to the note she clutched in her hand. She had to blink away the tears in her eyes in order to read it.

Detective,
As you can see by the photo I took of your girlfriend, she's not doing well. I'm trying to decide if it wouldn't be better to simply kill her without making the exchange we discussed. I'll let you know tomorrow what I've decided.

It wasn't signed, but then again Kay hadn't expected it to be. She handed it back to Paul.

"Where's Max?" Kay stared at the front door and refused to look at any of them. Rayne wanted her. He wouldn't kill Brenda without doing it somewhere where he could see her pain as he did it. She'd been dealing with scumbags like this for years, and she knew how they worked. He was all about instant gratification. Killing Brenda without being able to witness Kay's pain wouldn't give it to him.

"We went back in and took him to our house when you left this morning," Fran said. "I'll have Michael bring him back now."

"I'm staying here tonight," Quinn said sternly.

"No, you're not," Kay said, finally meeting his gaze. "Fran and Michael are enough, and Max will be here. He won't come back anyway, and you know it."

Kay went into the house without another word, but Quinn followed her. She went to the kitchen and poured herself a glass of scotch. She held the bottle out to him, but he shook his head.

"Griff, you aren't really going to give yourself in exchange for Brenda, are you?"

"Of course I am."

"I'm trying to put any one of us in her position, and I don't see you making this deal for anyone else. You're acting desperate, Kay."

"Well, you know what they say—desperate times call for desperate measures. He's backed me into a corner, and I don't have a choice but to fight back, Larry." Kay downed the liquid from her glass and slammed it onto the counter. "For the first time in my life I've found someone to truly care about. I *will not* let him take that away from me."

"Honey, come on," Fran said when everyone was gone. She led Kay to the living room and got her situated on the couch. "Michael will be here any minute. I'm making you some soup. Do you want a sandwich too?"

"No," Kay sobbed, holding on to her. Fran held her tightly as they sat there, and rocked slowly back and forth, stroking Kay's hair.

"Shhh," Fran whispered to her. "Shhh, Kay. Everything's going to be all right."

"Will it?" Kay asked, not believing her friend. She sat up and leaned back to look at her. "If that bastard kills her, nothing will ever be all right again, Fran."

"Your colleagues said he wouldn't do that," Fran reminded her. "He's just using her to get to you. If he were to kill her, he would lose his leverage. If you stop believing it now, you'll only succeed in driving yourself crazy."

Kay knew she was right, but it didn't make the threats in his note any easier to take. She finally nodded and motioned for Fran to go make the soup. When she was gone, Kay looked out the window to the street in front of her house. She sighed when she saw Quinn and Elam backed into the driveway across the street. It didn't surprise her they were there, but it made her wonder. Did they really think Rayne would show up again, or were they more worried she'd go out looking for him?

When the doorbell rang, Kay jumped to her feet, her weapon drawn before she could even think about what she was doing. Fran came out of the kitchen and looked at her. The rational part of Kay's brain told her Quinn and Elam would never have allowed Rayne to get to her front door; therefore, whoever it was couldn't be a threat. The irrational part of her brain told her it was Tommy Rayne coming to taunt her face-to-face.

"It's probably just Michael," Fran said. If she was frightened by Kay's reaction to the doorbell, she hid it well. She started toward the door. "Put the gun away and go eat some soup."

"Fran, wait," Kay said as she went to stand between her and the door. "You don't know for sure it's Michael."

"You're overreacting." Fran tried to push past her, but Kay gripped her arm hard. She looked at the hand squeezing her biceps before meeting Kay's gaze. "I'll let this go because I know you're under a lot of stress, Kay, but be reasonable. Do you honestly think he'd show up and ring the doorbell?"

"Kay, it's Gary and Laura Jansen!" Gary called out before pounding on the front door. Kay released Fran as she slammed the gun back into its shoulder holster.

"Is there any news?" Laura asked when Kay opened the door for them. Kay glanced across the street to see Quinn still parked in the neighbor's driveway. She ushered Brenda's parents inside and locked the door behind them. "You talked to him tonight, didn't you?"

"Yes, a little while ago. He's going to contact us again tomorrow evening," Kay said, wondering why the hell Quinn hadn't called to warn her about her visitors. She wasn't up to this now. They followed her into the living room and took seats on the couch. She wasn't sure whether to tell them about the phone Rayne left in her house, but ultimately decided they needed to know. Kay watched as Fran went back to the kitchen and she began to recount the evening's events for the Jansens.

"But she's alive, right?" Gary asked when she'd told them about the photo on Brenda's phone. He was holding tightly to his wife's hand. "You spoke to her after the picture was taken?"

"Yes, I did. Hours after the picture was taken." Kay looked at her phone when it vibrated on her hip, a message from Quinn to tell her Michael was almost to her front door. She also noticed the earlier text telling her the Jansens were there. Apparently, she'd been so wrapped up in her thoughts she hadn't noticed it. She waved Fran to answer it when he rang the bell. "She sounded fine when I spoke with her. She was lucid, and was able to assure me she wasn't badly hurt."

"What if he kills her?" Laura asked, her voice choked. "I don't know if I could survive that."

"He won't kill her," Kay said.

"How can you be so sure?" Gary asked. "He had to have some reason for abducting her. How can you know what his endgame is?"

Kay almost shook her head and began to tell a lie, but it was time to tell these people the real reason behind their daughter's abduction.

"It's me he wants. He won't kill her because his endgame is to kill me," she said quickly, before she had the chance to stop herself. The ensuing silence was awkward, but Gary finally met her eyes.

"This is because you broke his nose?"

"Apparently, I humiliated him when I did that," Kay said. "His vendetta is with me, and I'm afraid Brenda was a convenient way to get me to do what he wants. He's calling tomorrow to set up a time and place to exchange her for me."

"This is crazy," Laura said, her voice barely above a whisper.

"Listen, I'm sure you hate me right now, but I love Brenda," Kay said. For some reason, she needed them to know this. "I love her with all I am, and I can assure you we are going to do everything we can to get her back safely."

"Including giving your own life for hers?" Gary asked, the shock evident in his voice and his expression. "That's ridiculous, Kay, and we don't hate you. You can't seriously be considering an exchange?"

"Our hope is it won't get that far. We plan to have people in place to get a clean shot at him once he releases Brenda. But if we can't, then yes, I'm prepared to give myself up for Brenda's safety."

The Jansens just looked at each other for a moment before getting up and saying their good-byes. They insisted she call them when she knew anything else, and then they left. Kay assumed they were in shock. She'd expected accusations of putting Brenda in danger against her will, but they said nothing bad about her. That somehow made her feel worse than if they had blamed her for this.

CHAPTER TWENTY-SEVEN

It was true if Tommy killed the little dyke, it would most assuredly succeed in hurting Griffith. But it wouldn't give him nearly the satisfaction he desired. The pleasure he could only get if he were to be able to give the bitch the news himself. Or when he killed Griffith. That was what he really wanted to do, and anything else would feel like failure.

Tommy smiled to himself. The cot he was on wasn't the most relaxing place in the world to sleep, but he was damn sure he was more comfortable than the dyke in the basement was. At least he wasn't lying on the cement floor.

So no, he concluded, it would not be in his best interest to let Brenda die. He decided to stick with the original plan, and trade her for Griffith. He got up from the cot and grabbed a rag and a bottle of hydrogen peroxide before he headed back down to the basement to clean up the wound on the side of her head. If she showed up for the exchange with blood covering her face, Griffith might go ballistic.

Brenda opened her eyes when she heard Rayne fumbling with the lock, but she was forced to close them again when the harsh fluorescents above her assaulted her eyes. Continuous blinking was the only way she could adjust to the lights. Brenda had been worried ever since he'd left that he might come to the realization if he were to kill her, it would hurt Kay far worse than if he were to kill Kay herself.

She decided she couldn't think that way. Her goal right now was to stay alive long enough to speak to Kay again, and give her a clue as to where she was being held. Then if he did end up killing her, at least Kay might still be able to catch him.

Brenda wondered if Rayne knew she could hear the music coming from above. Anytime he had turned the light on, it had been a good minute before he made it to where she was, and the piped in music was already playing by the time he came in. Perhaps he wasn't even aware of it, which would make it even easier for her to give Kay a vague message about it.

Brenda flinched involuntarily when he grabbed her and roughly rolled her onto her back, which caused considerable pain in her shoulder. She refused to cry out, and instead bit her lip. She was surprised to see he had a bottle of peroxide and a semi-clean cloth in his hands, and he was acting as though he intended to clean her wounds.

"I decided I'd better clean you up," he said gruffly. "Wouldn't want this to get infected now, would we?"

"Thank you," she said quietly. He looked surprised at her gratitude, but went about his task at hand.

"This is pretty bad," he said. He grimaced, which worried Brenda a bit. "You're going to need stitches. I don't think I can stop it from bleeding, but I can clean it. You aren't losing so much blood it'll kill you, and hopefully you'll be in a hospital soon. If your girlfriend goes through with the exchange, that is."

Brenda must have looked surprised, because Tommy laughed.

"Oh, I seriously considered killing you, but don't worry. That isn't my real objective," he assured her. "Gotta keep my eye on the prize. She's the one I want dead, and we all know that, don't we?"

Seriously? Keep his *eye* on the prize? Brenda didn't answer him because she was afraid she'd begin laughing hysterically at his pun, intended or not. As he continued to try to clean her wound, she could feel the flap of skin on her scalp and it scared her. It felt as if a very large part of her scalp had been torn away from the skull. She couldn't help but wince in pain, and when she did, he truly looked apologetic for doing this to her.

"There," he said finally. He turned her back onto her other side and then picked up his things. "It's the best I can do. I'll bring you some food in the morning."

"Why are you waiting until tomorrow night to call her again?" Brenda asked. She closed her eyes so she wouldn't have to look at him.

"What?"

"Why are you dragging this out for so long? You could call her in the morning and this could all be over before tomorrow night." She tried desperately not to think about the exchange he was planning. She had to believe Kay had contingencies in place.

"What fun would there be in that?" he asked. "She needs to suffer before I end this. Worrying about what's happening with you is the best way to accomplish that, don't you think?"

"Are you sure you've had enough to eat?" Fran asked as Kay pushed the bowl away. "I can fix you something else."

"I don't want anything else," she replied distractedly. "I want to get drunk. Do you want to get drunk with me? I finished what little scotch there was, but I think I have some whiskey somewhere."

"Kay, I'm not sure that's a good idea," Fran said with obvious concern.

"Fran, you're my dearest friend, and I love you to pieces," Kay said as she stood from the kitchen table and began rummaging through cupboards in search of the elusive whiskey bottle. *Where the hell did I put it?* "The woman I'm in love with has been abducted, and God only knows what she's going through right now. She said she wasn't badly hurt, but I don't believe her. Not only because of the blood in the picture, but how else would Rayne be able to get her to go with him? She doesn't strike me as being a weak person, Fran. I think she only told me that so I wouldn't worry too much about her."

Kay said a silent cheer when she found the bottle, way in the back of the cupboard above the refrigerator. Damn, she thought. There wasn't as much left as she thought there was. Certainly not enough to get drunk on. She took it with her to the table anyway.

"Do you want some?" she asked as she sat down again, but Fran and Michael both shook their heads. She removed the top and took a drink straight from the bottle.

"Kay, are you sure that's a good idea?" Michael asked.

"Seriously? Do you remember how many times we got drunk when we were younger?"

"Yeah, and it was a bad idea then too."

"Bullshit. It's a brilliant idea. And if the liquor stores weren't closed, I'd go out and buy more because do you have any idea how stressful it was having to tell her parents I was responsible for their daughter being abducted?"

"It wasn't your fault, Kay. You said you gave her an out before your relationship started," Michael said, always the voice of reason.

"They don't know that," Kay said with a dismissive wave of her hand. "They were in shock when they left here."

"Give them the benefit of the doubt, Kay," Fran said. "They seem like sensible people to me. And any sane person would realize this was because Rayne is unstable, not because you said or did something to push him over the edge."

"It's almost eleven, Kay. I think you should get some sleep." Michael was trying to do the right thing, and Kay loved him for it. But did they honestly think she'd be able to get any sleep?

"Later."

"What time is he supposed to call tomorrow?" Michael asked. Kay looked at him and wondered briefly if she should be jealous. Max was sitting by his side, his chin resting on Michael's thigh.

"Five p.m.," Kay answered. "So it doesn't matter if I go to bed now or at four in the morning."

"I still think you should go to bed sooner than later." Michael could really be annoying when he wanted to be.

"I only have those shows on television to go by, but isn't it odd he's drawing this out so much?" Fran asked. "Why not get it over with as soon as possible?"

"He's playing with me." Kay took the last drink of whiskey and set the bottle down on the table. "Statistics would show it isn't normal, you're right. But we aren't dealing with someone normal. For Rayne, I'm nothing but a lab rat he can force to play his twisted game. As long as he's getting pleasure from jerking me around, he'll keep doing it."

She was getting a headache from the all the stress and she decided maybe she should try to get some sleep. She rinsed out the whiskey bottle and made her way upstairs, Max right on her heels. Michael and Fran followed her up on the way to her guest room. Even though she was certain Rayne wouldn't show up at her house again, it made her feel better to know she wasn't alone.

CHAPTER TWENTY-EIGHT

K ay awoke in the morning with a blistering headache. She wasn't entirely sure if it was from the alcohol or because she hadn't been able to sleep for longer than twenty minutes at a time. She got out of the bed with a glance at the clock. Eight thirty. Only eight and a half more hours to wait for his damned phone call. After showering, she grabbed her cell phone and made her way down to the kitchen.

She'd looked on Brenda's phone last night before Paul took it as evidence, assuming she'd be able to find Dana's number, but if it was there, Brenda had given a different name to it. She wasn't about to start calling all the numbers in the phone with a two-one-five area code, but she really wanted to get in touch with Dana. Kay thought not only should she know what was going on, but she also might have some idea as to where Rayne might be. It was a long shot, she knew, but she was merely grasping at straws at this point. She'd never felt so helpless in her life.

As she sat outside with a cup of coffee, she called Paul.

"Webber," he said.

"It's Kay," she said. "I want to get into Brenda's apartment."

"Elam and Becker were already there for most of the day yesterday, Kay. We got all the evidence that was there."

"I know, Paul, but I want to get her address book, if she has one," Kay explained. "I need to get in touch with the lead singer of her band."

"Could she possibly help us?"

"Maybe," Kay replied and then sighed as she ran a hand through her hair. "Probably not, but I want to talk to her anyway."

"All right, I'll have Quinn meet you over there. It's still taped off as a crime scene so things should still be just as she left them," he said. After a pause, he asked, "How did you sleep last night?"

"Not well," Kay admitted. "Pretty shitty, if you want to know the truth. Every time I'd fall asleep, I'd dream about her, and then I'd be awake again. I'll be fine after a couple of cups of coffee."

"I'll send Quinn now. He should be there in about thirty minutes."

"Thanks, Paul," she said before hanging up.

She decided she'd better wake Michael and Fran up, at least to tell them she was leaving. She didn't want them to wake up and find she was gone. No doubt they would think she went out looking for Rayne herself.

Brenda woke up when Rayne hoisted her roughly into the chair again. She was finding it increasingly difficult to stay awake on her own. He set a fast food bag on her lap before moving behind her in order to untie her hands. The move surprised her, but when he came around to face her again, he had his gun in his hand.

"I know you're probably too weak to try anything stupid, but why take chances?" he asked as he sat and watched her slowly eat the breakfast he had gotten her.

It was difficult to chew, which was probably thanks to the backhand he had given her the day before. She was pretty sure nothing was broken, but her jaw hurt every time she tried to bite down. Normally, she loathed fast food breakfast, but she hadn't eaten anything in so long the lukewarm sandwich tasted wonderful.

"You probably didn't think I'd feed you this morning, did you?" he asked, and Brenda only shook her head slightly. He laughed. "I've decided when we'll make the exchange, but I still need to figure out where. Any suggestions?"

Was he serious? Asking her for suggestions?

"How about hell?" she asked before she could stop her mouth from reacting. She expected him to hit her again, but he only laughed.

"You're feisty *and* funny," he said, shaking his head. "I think perhaps I'm beginning to understand what she sees in you."

Yeah, right, she thought to herself. She managed to stop herself before she laughed. Instead, she just choked on what she was trying to swallow. He took the rest of the food away from her and handed her a bottle of water, which she downed in one drink. She knew she shouldn't have—the one thing he hadn't done for her was let her go to the bathroom. As near as she could tell, there wasn't even one in this room. As a result, she had urinated on herself more than once. At least the smell of it helped to cover up the stench of what she was now convinced was rotting flesh.

After he tied her hands again, he laid her back down on the floor.

"Rest up," he said cheerfully. "We have a very important phone call to make this evening."

Kay got to Brenda's apartment building early and ended up having to wait in her car for Larry to show up. Waiting had never been a strong point, and it was even less so now. All it did was give her more time to think about what she *couldn't* do to help Brenda. She sat there wishing she could talk to her. She would give anything to hold her in her arms again. As more time went by, she became increasingly worried Rayne would decide to kill Brenda instead of making the deal.

Kay was about to call Quinn to see what was taking him so damn long when she saw Dana pull into the parking lot. Her heart leapt in her chest as Kay silently hoped God would see fit to answer her other prayers as well in the coming hours.

"Dana!" she yelled as they both got out of their cars. Dana turned to look at her and smiled as she waved, and then began walking toward her. Quinn finally pulled in as she and Dana reached each other.

"I thought you and Brenda were leaving yesterday," Dana said in confusion, giving her a brief hug. "Is she inside?"

"No," Kay replied, and glanced over at Quinn as he approached them. She motioned in his direction before showing Dana her badge. She was pretty sure Brenda would have told Dana she was a cop, but figured it wouldn't hurt to reiterate the point. "This is my partner, Larry Quinn. Larry, this is Dana."

"What's going on?" Dana asked.

"Let's go upstairs to her apartment, and we can talk for a few minutes," Kay suggested as she cupped Dana's elbow in her hand and began walking toward the building.

"Where's Brenda?" she asked, obviously becoming alarmed. She stopped in her tracks when Kay and Quinn just looked at each other, but didn't answer. "Kay, she's my best friend. Tell me what the hell is going on."

"Tommy Rayne has her," Kay said quietly as she forced Dana to walk again. "He wants to exchange her for me. We came here today so we could try and find your phone number. I wanted to get in touch with you, to let you know what was happening. Also, I was hoping you might be able to help us."

"Help you with what?" she asked skeptically as she fumbled with her keys to unlock the door to the apartment. Quinn told her to ignore the crime scene tape blocking the door, and it was obvious she was shaken. "I'm not sure I know anything that could help."

Kay tried not to notice the blood on the floor right inside the door. She tried to convince herself it had been a superficial wound, since Brenda had seemed to be alert and awake when she had spoken to her last night.

"Do you know Tommy Rayne?" Kay asked her as she watched while Dana fed the fish. Kay had only been in the apartment a couple of times, but she could see Brenda everywhere she looked. She took a deep breath and felt Quinn's steadying hand on the small of her back.

"I've never talked to him, if that's what you mean," Dana said. She finally turned to look at them, and Kay saw she was crying. "He's an asshole, and I never wanted anything to do with him. He seemed to get his jollies by standing in front of his store and yelling at all the women going in and out of Discovery."

"Did you ever see him anywhere other than his shop?" Quinn asked after it became apparent Kay was too choked up to speak. He used his best calm-the-victim voice, and it seemed to soothe Dana a little. Kay was surprised it was working to soothe her nerves as well. Quinn was always so much better with people than she was.

"I don't know. I guess he came into the bar a couple of times for a drink," she said after spending a moment thinking about it. "Carol hated him being there, but she always took his money without a problem."

"Anywhere else?" Kay asked when she finally managed to find her voice again. "Please think about this for a minute. Anything you can tell us may help."

Dana stood there for what seemed like forever to Kay and finally shook her head. Her expression told Kay she thought she was hurting Brenda by not being able to help. Kay went to her and held her in her arms as Quinn excused himself and stepped out into the hallway to give them a few minutes alone.

"I'm so sorry," Dana sobbed, and Kay thought it ironic she was the one doing the comforting in this situation.

"It's okay," she said. Dana pushed away from her and wiped her eyes. "We will find her, Dana, and she'll be all right."

"Oh God, she must have been on the phone with me when he got here yesterday," Dana said quietly. "We thought maybe it was you at the door, and she hung up with me. She said you guys were leaving on a vacation yesterday."

"That was the plan," Kay said.

"I wasn't very happy she was leaving with no notice," Dana said, shaking her head. "The band was her idea to begin with. I had to make a lot of phone calls yesterday to try and find a decent fill-in for her."

"Did you find one?" Kay asked as they headed for the door. Talking about something else was probably good for both of them.

"Yeah, and we had to have an emergency rehearsal session last night to get her familiar with the music." She locked the door behind them as they walked into the hallway. They started walking back to the parking lot. "We have to have another one tonight. Will you call me if you get any news on her?"

"I will," Kay promised, and asked her to write down her number. The piece of paper she got back from her had three numbers—her home, work, and cell phone. Kay gave Dana her own cell phone number and asked her to call if she thought of anything that might help.

"I think she made a good choice with you," Dana said. "I mean, you seem to really care about her, and that's important, you know?"

"Yeah, I do know." Kay smiled and nodded her head before pulling Dana into another embrace. "And I do care about her very much."

Kay spent the rest of the day doing her best to not lose her mind. She didn't seem to be doing a very good job of it though. Paul and Larry both tried to keep the mood lighthearted, but they weren't succeeding in their endeavor either. She did appreciate their efforts though.

After they arrived back at the station from Brenda's apartment building, the time seemed to drag. Finally, at three, Larry convinced her they should go out and get something to eat. She made him promise they would be back in time for her to receive Rayne's phone call.

Larry had always been like a brother to her since she'd made detective, and there were times she honestly didn't know what she'd have done without him. The incident when she'd broken Rayne's nose was a good indicator of that fact. He'd been there for her throughout the entire ordeal.

It was true he'd not tried very hard to stop her as she slammed the butt of her gun into Rayne's face, but he was the one who got her out of there before the press and Internal Affairs arrived at the scene. He stood up for her where IA was concerned. By making it clear to them Rayne had deserved what he'd gotten, she was convinced he had everything to do with her not getting a longer suspension. Or possibly even being dismissed from duty altogether.

Kay was more than a little worried about what Paul was going to have to face when this was all over. She was sure IA would be all over his ass about bringing her back to work the case when she was technically still out on suspension. It touched her to realize he didn't seem to give a damn about what might happen to him down the road. All he cared about was getting Brenda back safe and nailing Rayne for kidnapping Brenda and for killing the woman two days ago. It still irked her they couldn't find the evidence to charge him with the murders of the first two women though.

"Kay, you look totally stressed out," Larry said as they headed back to the station. "Are you sure you're going to be all right to talk to him when he calls?"

Kay glanced at her watch and then shook her head. Only half an hour to go. As she laid her head back against the seat, she said, "No, but do you think it's going to stop me?"

"No," he answered, and laughed as he shook his head. "The only thing that's ever stopped you is being out on suspension. I don't think there's much of anything that could keep you down for long."

"I think losing Brenda might just succeed in keeping me down," Kay admitted. She stared out the passenger side window. She wasn't sure why she felt so strongly about Brenda after such a relatively short amount of time. It didn't seem possible she should. All she knew was she did, and there wasn't anybody who could change her mind about it.

"You aren't going to lose her," Larry said with assurance, placing his hand on her leg and squeezing gently for emphasis. "I know you better than most people do, Kay, and if there's any way at all you can save her, I know you will. I have confidence in your abilities, and I know Paul does too, or else he wouldn't be putting his ass on the line for you."

She thanked him as he pulled into the lot and turned off the engine. They exited the car and made their way to the elevator as she looked at her watch for what seemed like the millionth time that day and sighed. Twenty more minutes.

CHAPTER TWENTY-NINE

Don't you dare pass out on me again, dyke," Rayne said gruffly as he grabbed Brenda by the front of the shirt and shook her. Her head felt like it was being slammed against a wall. She opened her eyes, and mercifully, he stopped shaking her. "If your girlfriend doesn't talk to you when I call her, she might be inclined to believe I killed you. Trust me when I say it would be bad for both of you."

"What time is it?" Brenda asked. She was having trouble keeping her head up. Her chin kept wanting to rest on her chest. It was because he insisted on putting her in this damned chair. Why couldn't he just leave her on the ground? It was painful sure, but at least she didn't feel like gravity was trying to do a number on her body.

Before he'd gotten down here, she'd heard the music again. Her band. She knew for certain now that it was them. Knowing it made her anxious to speak with Kay, but she kept closing her eyes to try to hide from him the fact that she thought she knew where he was keeping her.

"Why? Got a hot date?" He laughed at his own joke and Brenda wanted to punch him in the throat. Or kick him in the groin. Either option would be satisfying as hell, but she knew she didn't have the strength to do either, even if he were to untie her and give her a free shot.

She tried not to look too impatient as he pulled out a cell phone and started dialing. If he had any clue as to what she was thinking he'd never allow her to speak with Kay, so she kept her eyes down and tried not to fidget in her seat.

"Here we go," he said with a sickening grin. He pressed the call button and held the phone to his ear, never taking his eye off Brenda.

"Let me talk to her," Kay said when she answered on the first ring, her voice once again coming through loud and clear. "I need to know she's still all right."

"I don't think you're in a position to be making demands, Detective," he said, laughing.

"You said I could talk to her, Tommy. Please." Kay sounded so distraught Brenda had to swallow hard in order not to cry out to her. "I got your little gift last night. If you don't let me talk to her, there will be no exchange."

"Fine," he said. As he took the phone from his ear, he met Brenda's eyes, and there was an explicit warning there for her. He didn't show her the gun this time, but she had to assume he had it. She saw the look he gave her, and he knew she'd seen it. He held the phone to her ear.

"Kay?" she said weakly.

"Brenda, are you all right?" she asked. At least she didn't start crying this time, like she had the night before.

"Tired," she said, still staring into Rayne's one eye. She said a silent prayer before adding, "Can you get a message to Dana for me? Tell her I'm sorry I missed rehearsal last night and tonight."

"Honey, what are you talking about?" Kay sounded confused, and Brenda hoped to God she would figure out what she was trying to tell her. "We weren't even going to be around."

"I know, but I didn't get a chance to tell her, and she'll be upset I wasn't there," Brenda managed to say before Rayne pulled the phone from her ear.

"Enough," he said to both of them.

He began walking around the room, and Brenda finally lost the fight of trying to keep her head up. She felt drool coming from the corner of her mouth. At least she hoped it was drool, and not more blood.

"Tommy," Kay said calmly, although she was feeling anything but. She snapped her fingers and waved her hand furiously to get Paul's attention from where he was across the squad room listening in on the conversation. Brenda had to have been giving her a clue. When Paul looked her way, she waved for him to hurry up. She wrote one word on the tablet of paper before her—Discovery—and underlined it several times. "I can't do anything for you until you tell me what it is you want."

"I want you dead, and for me to be the one who kills you," he answered angrily. The one thing Kay didn't want was for him to lose control of his emotions.

"I need to know where you want to make the exchange," Kay said. "I'll need to bring one other officer with me, but he'll only be there to take Brenda, so she can get checked out medically. You have my word; once you turn her over, I will go with you, and no one will follow."

"What good is your word to me?" he asked.

"It's all you have, Tommy," she pointed out. "What good is your word to me that she'll be returned unharmed?"

"Fine," he said impatiently. "Tomorrow morning. Nine o'clock. At the front gate of Lincoln Financial Field." He hung up without another word to her.

"Fucking asshole," Kay said into the dead connection. She grabbed the gun from her desk and slammed it in her shoulder holster. Paul and Larry were standing there waiting. "We need to go to Discovery."

"Why? You already talked to the owner, right?" Paul asked.

"I think Brenda was trying to give me a clue as to where he's holding her," Kay said as they headed to the elevator. Becker and Elam were right behind them. "She wouldn't have known Dana scheduled emergency rehearsals for the band to get their new drummer familiar with the music. She has to be somewhere she can hear them playing."

"Do you honestly think he would be so bold as to keep her there?" Paul asked as they sped down the road to the bar. Elam was driving his own car and seemed to have no problem keeping up with them. At Kay's insistence, neither car used lights or sirens. If she was right, she didn't want Rayne knowing they were showing up.

"Bold?" she asked, shaking her head. "I think it was more of a calculated risk on his part. He knew we would search his apartment and the pawnshop first, and then we probably wouldn't come back. Why not keep her somewhere we've already been? It makes perfect sense to me. I just don't know why we didn't think of it before."

"I don't know, Kay," he said doubtfully.

"Worst case scenario, I misunderstood what she was trying to tell me," Kay said. She checked the clip in her gun for the hundredth time. She had so much nervous energy she didn't know what to do with it. "If that's the case, then we have to wait for the exchange in the morning. Best case, she told me where she is, and he has absolutely no clue we're on our way. Either way, I can't sit on my hands and do nothing, Paul."

Rayne tied a rope around Brenda's chest in order to keep her upright in the chair and placed a new piece of tape over her mouth. He then left the room without another word. Brenda heard him snapping the padlock shut again. A moment later, the lights and classical music were gone.

She sat there in the darkness listening to the band play from somewhere above her. There was a distant thought in her head that the drummer Dana had found to replace her wasn't half bad.

She prayed Kay got the meaning in what she had said. She kept listening for any lapse in the beat that might indicate Kay and the troops had shown up. The more time that passed, the less hope Brenda held on to. After a few minutes, the music stopped, but then it started again, without Dana singing. Hoping it meant Kay had arrived, Brenda's adrenaline kicked in, and she frantically tried one more time to get her hands free.

❖

Kay's step faltered when they walked into the bar and saw what looked like a wedding reception going on. Carol didn't look too happy as she walked over to the five of them.

"Have you found Brenda?" Carol asked.

"No, we haven't. Detective Becker, Detective Elam, and Lieutenant Webber, this is Carol, and you've already met Detective Quinn" Kay said quickly. There was no time for this. "Where's Dana and the band? I thought they were rehearsing tonight."

"I couldn't let them practice here tonight because of this private event. They use one of the band member's house for rehearsal sometimes."

"Where is that?" Quinn asked.

"I don't know. Camden, I think. I could call Dana if you need me to."

"I can call her." Kay turned and left the bar as she pulled her cell out and hit speed dial for the number she'd stored in the phone earlier in the day. It rang four times before going to voicemail. She left a message for Dana to return her call immediately and then fought the urge to throw the phone as she swore out loud.

"Kay?" Paul said from beside her.

"She probably couldn't hear the phone because they're rehearsing," she said turning toward Rayne's pawnshop. "Let's go talk to Billy."

She quickly walked inside without bothering to see if they were following her. Billy stood from behind the counter and looked like he was scared to death.

"He isn't here," Billy said quickly.

"I know," Kay said, never slowing her stride until she reached the counter. "I need you to tell me where he is, Billy. He's going to kill a woman if you don't help us now."

Billy swallowed hard and looked at the intimidating presence she'd brought with her. He started shuffling through some papers and seemed to panic when he couldn't find what he was looking for.

"Where is he?" Quinn asked, his voice booming.

Billy jumped back and shook his head. "He called earlier today and asked me to bring him something after I closed up tonight. I can't find the paper I wrote the address down on."

"Billy, I'm disappointed," Kay said, her voice much calmer than she felt. "Didn't you promise me you'd call me as soon as you heard anything from him?"

"I lost your number."

"Where is he?" Quinn asked again.

"I don't know the address, I swear."

"Is he in the city?" Paul asked from behind her.

"Camden," Billy said as he shook his head and put his hands up in front of him. "That's all I can remember."

"Call him," Kay said.

"I can't. He called from a burner and said he was tossing it as soon as we hung up."

Paul took Quinn aside as Elam and Becker went behind the counter and helped him look for the address. Kay went to where Paul and Quinn were but never took her eyes from Billy.

"It's still a couple of hours before he's going to close for the night," Quinn said.

"Then that gives us time to get things set up. We're going to be the ones knocking on the door tonight. Rayne will think it's Billy so he won't hesitate to open the door. When he does, the bastard will have five guns pointed at his head," Paul said. "Billy will be with us just in case he asks who it is before he opens the door. I'm going to call Camden police and set things up with them. Someone stays with Billy the entire time. I don't want him trying to contact Rayne to let him know what's up."

Quinn nodded once and then Paul left to make some calls.

"Are you all right, Griff?"

"I will be when we have the fucker in custody and Brenda's safe."

CHAPTER THIRTY

Billy was nervous as hell as they made their way to the back of the house where Rayne had instructed him to go. He stood in front of the door and waited while everyone got into place. Kay stood far enough to his right so Rayne wouldn't see her if he made a quick check from the window in the door. Quinn took up the same place to Billy's left. Camden's PD had sent a sharpshooter Kay hoped to God they wouldn't need. Paul, Becker, Elam, and a handful of Camden uniformed officers were a few feet back in the bushes. Kay's heart felt as though it might beat right out of her chest.

After a quick glance to make sure everyone was ready, Kay gave Billy a nod. She and Quinn had their weapons ready. Billy knocked loudly and took a nervous step away from the door as they had instructed him to do. A moment later, they heard footsteps from inside the house.

"Who is it?" Rayne asked as he peeked through the curtain.

"Billy," he answered.

The curtain closed and Kay heard the deadbolt being unlocked. She spared a quick look at Quinn who trained his weapon in the approximate area Rayne's head would be once the door opened. Since it opened from Kay's side, Quinn would have the first look at him. Kay heard the other detectives and officers taking up a position at the bottom of the steps and didn't have to look to know they all had their weapons pointed at the door as Quinn pushed Billy out of the way.

"It's about time—" Rayne didn't have the chance to finish his sentence before he looked up and saw Quinn's gun a few inches from his face. "What the fuck, Billy!"

Rayne tried to slam the door shut but Quinn had his foot in the way so it only bounced back open. Kay followed Quinn inside in time to see Rayne reaching for the gun he had tucked into the front of his jeans.

"Don't even think about it," Kay said. Rayne watched her intently for a moment before a slow smile began to take over his features. He got the gun out but held it to his side. "Drop it, Tommy. This is over now."

"It's not over until I make you pay for what you did to me," he said with a sneer. "Nobody gets away with making fun of me."

"Is that why you killed those prostitutes?" Quinn asked, the weapon never moving from where he had it pointed between Rayne's eyes. "They made fun of you?"

"Them, my mother," he said nodding. Kay saw him slowly raising his arm in her direction and she readied herself to have to shoot. He looked at Kay. "But you did it in front of other people, bitch. You won't get away with it."

"Drop your weapon, Rayne. This is the last warning!" Quinn said. Before Rayne could even think to get it aimed anywhere a shot would do fatal damage, Quinn shot him in the chest. Rayne looked surprised as his body slammed back against the wall, but he didn't drop the gun. When he tried to raise his arm again, Quinn shot him in the hand. As soon as he hit the floor, everyone rushed into the house.

Kay took off through the house looking for Brenda. They could deal with Rayne without her help. She pulled open a door off what she assumed would be the dining room had the house been occupied and found another door behind it. It was secured with two padlocks.

"Kay?" Elam asked from behind her.

"I need the keys for this. He has to have them in his pocket somewhere."

She brushed past Elam on her way back to the kitchen, not stopping until she knelt down in front of Rayne who was slumped against the wall. He was unconscious and bleeding a lot. She'd never wished death on anyone before, but she did now. She heard someone calling for an ambulance as she found the keys in his shirt pocket and hurried back to open the door.

"Get Paul," she called over her shoulder when she got the door open. Her heart was pounding so hard she could hear little else. The stench of rotting human flesh hit her nostrils with such ferocity she came close to losing what little she'd eaten that day. She tried to ignore it as she hurried down the stairs into the basement.

She almost dropped to her knees when she saw Brenda sitting in a chair, her back to Kay. Brenda was trying frantically to get her hands untied, but stopped and was trying to look over her shoulder when she heard someone coming down the steps. Obviously, she was worried it might be Rayne coming back.

Kay ran over and knelt in front of her, tears flowing freely now. Paul and Elam came rushing down the steps and began to work on untying Brenda's wrists and ankles as Kay gently pulled the tape from her mouth. Brenda was crying too, and when her hands were free, she hugged Kay tightly.

"Brenda," Kay murmured as she leaned back to get a good look at her. She reached out but stopped short of touching the wound on Brenda's head. She worked hard to keep her expression neutral so as not to worry Brenda about how bad it looked. "What did he do to you, baby?"

"It doesn't matter now," Brenda said, sobbing. "I was so afraid I'd never see you again."

"Can you stand up?" Kay asked as she got to her feet and tried to help her get out of the chair. Paul and Jack were on the other side of the room now, apparently to give them a moment alone.

"I don't think I can," Brenda said after giving it a try and falling back into a sitting position.

"Ambulance?" Kay asked Paul, and he nodded, indicating they were already on their way. When he turned away again, Kay kissed Brenda on the lips. "You're going to be fine, baby, and when you get out of the hospital, we're going away for a while, all right?"

Brenda nodded, but it was apparent she was having trouble focusing. The adrenaline that no doubt kept her going was finally fading away and she passed out in Kay's arms.

"Oh, my God," Dana said from the doorway just as Brenda's body slumped. She ran to them. "Is she…?"

"Passed out from exhaustion, but alive," Kay assured her quickly as she felt for Brenda's pulse, and found it beating weakly, but at least it was beating. Knowing Brenda was finally safe, Kay allowed herself to calm a bit. "What are you doing in here? This is a crime scene. They shouldn't have let you in."

"I saw your partner outside and he told me what was going on. He let me in." Dana kept looking at Brenda worriedly. "We were rehearsing next door at a friend's house."

Kay saw the paramedics coming down the stairs behind Dana. "She's going to be all right, I promise. The ambulance is here, and I need you to move out of the way so they can get the stretcher in here."

Dana took a step back and watched as the paramedics checked Brenda out before putting her on the stretcher. Dana went to Kay without a word and hugged her tightly.

"Kay," Paul said, approaching them slowly. The paramedics were taking Brenda up the stairs. "You'd better go if you want to ride in the ambulance with her."

Dana let her go, and Kay went to hug Paul.

"Thank you," she said quietly, feeling the tears begin again, but this time they were tears of incredible relief. "For everything, Paul."

"You'll need to come down to the station later and give a statement," he said as he released her. "Given your history with Rayne, IA will no doubt be investigating the shooting. You're just lucky Quinn took the shot before you had the chance to."

Kay knew she owed not only her life, but Brenda's too, to her partner. She wasn't sure she would ever be able to repay him. She started up the steps after the stretcher but turned back to look at Paul.

"I'll lay odds there are more women buried down here, Paul. You can't mistake that smell for anything else. The bastard can't get away with it this time no matter how savvy his lawyer might be."

CHAPTER THIRTY-ONE

B renda's parents were at her bedside when Kay walked into her room in the early hours of the next morning. They both stood and motioned for her to come closer. Kay was grateful Paul had thought to call the Jansens, because the only thing she could think about was how quickly she could get to Brenda's bedside.

"How is she?" Kay asked. She'd wanted nothing more than to stay with Brenda until she woke up. After the ambulance arrived at the hospital, the doctor told her it would be a while before they were through with tests and she would be coherent enough to even know Kay was there, so she'd gone to the station to give her statement. "Has she come to yet?"

"About an hour ago," Laura said with a quick glance over her shoulder as they moved a little further away from the bed. "She asked for you before telling us a little of what happened to her and then she fell asleep again."

"We owe you and your entire department more than we can ever hope to repay you," Gary said. "You saved our little girl."

"If it hadn't been for me, this never would have happened to her in the first place," Kay said, feeling guilty for the gratitude these people were showing her.

"This was *his* fault, not yours. He made the choice to go after her. You can't blame yourself for any of it," Gary said. "We're just happy she's alive and Rayne will be rotting in prison."

Kay nodded, unsure of what to say. She didn't even try to stop her tears, and when Gary pulled her into an embrace, she cried harder. So *this* was what a loving family was like. She could get used to this. When he finally released her, Laura did the same. Kay took a shaky breath and went to Brenda.

"Kay?" Brenda said weakly. Kay eased herself to a sitting position on the mattress next to Brenda and took her hand gently. "You're here."

"Of course I am, baby." Kay answered as she brushed the hair back from Brenda's eyes. "Where else would I be?"

"You weren't here when I woke up before."

"I had to go in to the station and give a statement about what happened last night. About the shooting."

"Is Rayne dead?" she asked.

"He's here, in this hospital, on a different floor." Kay glanced at Brenda's parents, who were walking out the door. Apparently, they wanted to give them a few moments alone. "Honestly, they aren't sure at this point if he's going to make it. The bullet just missed his heart, but he lost a lot of blood before the medics could stabilize and transport him."

"Did you shoot him?" Brenda's expression seemed to brighten at the possibility. Kay couldn't help but laugh.

"No, I didn't. You remember my partner, Larry Quinn? You met him yesterday at the house." Kay paused and Brenda nodded. "He shot Rayne before Rayne could shoot me."

"Then we owe him a lot. Will he be in trouble because of this? If Rayne dies?"

"No. The statements we gave all proved it was a justified shooting. He'll have to go to some counseling sessions because he discharged his weapon and shot a human being, but there won't be any charges brought against him."

"Good. Then I hope Rayne doesn't make it. The man deserves to die after the things he did not only to me, but to those other women. There was a dead body in that room, wasn't there?"

"There's a team there now digging up the floor." Kay hadn't thought she'd be having this particular discussion with Brenda so soon after she woke up, but she took it as a positive sign Brenda was truly going to be okay mentally after her ordeal. "There wasn't a body, per se, but they've recovered some body parts. When those women were discovered in the Dumpsters, the only thing we never found were their feet, and the hearts he'd cut out of their chests. They were buried there."

"Was I under the bar?"

"No, you were in the basement of a house in Camden. But the clue you gave me sent us to Discovery, and then the kid running the pawnshop for Rayne helped us to get to you. It was brave of you, giving me that clue. Did he know what you'd done?"

"No."

Kay took a deep breath and let it out slowly. She didn't want to ask her next question, and she was sure Brenda had already spoken to the doctors and nurses about it, but Kay had to know.

"Baby, did he..." Kay's voice faltered, and she knew she couldn't ask it. She was relieved to realize Brenda knew what she was trying to say.

"He didn't touch me, if that's what you're asking." Brenda never looked away from her. "He didn't rape me."

"Thank God," Kay murmured.

"When can I go home?"

"Not for a couple of days," Kay said. She touched Brenda's cheek and then her hair. She couldn't seem to stop touching her. She was afraid she'd wake up any moment and realize Rayne had taken Brenda away from her. "You have a pretty bad concussion, and they needed almost thirty stitches to close the gash in your head. Whatever he hit you with ripped your scalp open pretty badly, but the doctor said you had a hard head. There was no damage to the skull."

"Lucky me," Brenda said. "My dad always said I was hard-headed. I guess he was right."

Brenda tentatively touched her scalp where the stitches were and her eyes went wide with surprise. She looked at Kay.

"They had to shave part of your head to stitch you up. It'll grow back, I promise."

"It's a small price to pay for both of us making it out alive."
Brenda grasped Kay's hand and held on to it tightly. "I was so
afraid I wouldn't be able to tell you in person that I love you."

Kay felt the tears threatening as she smiled at Brenda. She
wiped a tear from Brenda's cheek before leaning over and kissing
her on the lips.

"I love you, too. So much," she whispered, not fully trusting
her voice with this much emotion welling up inside her.

"Okay, the patient needs her rest," a nurse said as she came
striding quickly into the room. "You can come back later and see
her."

"Kay?" Brenda said as she gripped her hand when Kay
started to stand. Kay sat back down and placed a hand on Brenda's
cheek.

"What is it, baby?"

"I hope it's okay, but I asked my parents if we could use the
cottage for a couple of weeks when I'm well enough to travel."
Brenda smiled with a quick glance at the nurse. "I can't wait to
get you alone."

Kay glanced at the nurse too, but she seemed to be busy with
Brenda's medical chart. If she'd heard the declaration, she wasn't
giving any outward signs of it.

"It's more than all right," Kay said before leaning forward
and placing a kiss on Brenda's cheek. "Now hurry up and get
better so we can take an extended vacation."

"How extended?"

"Forever, if I have anything to say about it."

"What about your job?" Brenda asked, looking confused.

"I don't have a job any more. I turned in my badge and
weapon when I went to give my statement earlier. My time is my
own, as they say. I'll be back later to see you, all right?"

Brenda nodded, but Kay could tell she was full of questions.
Whether they were queries about Rayne, or about Kay quitting
the force she wasn't sure. But it didn't matter right then, because
they'd have all the time in the world to talk once Brenda was out
of the hospital.

CHAPTER THIRTY-TWO

Their trip to Canada was postponed for a few weeks while Brenda mended from her injuries. Kay had insisted she stay with her during her recovery, and she was grateful Gary and Laura agreed with her. They came every day and visited with both of them, and it seemed to help Brenda's mental state to have them around. They'd just left and Kay was standing in the bedroom doorway watching as Brenda, having gotten comfortable in the bed, was on her back with her eyes closed. She was wearing nothing but a T-shirt and a pair of boxers.

Kay smiled at the strangely gentle Max who was lying with her. He'd always slept at the foot of the bed since she'd gotten him, but now he was stretched out along Brenda's side, his chin resting gently on her shoulder. Brenda was smiling and scratching behind one of his ears. He hadn't left her side since Kay had brought her home from the hospital almost three weeks earlier.

"Are you going to join us, or do you want to just stand there staring at us?" Brenda asked after a few moments.

"Oh, I don't know. I kind of like seeing the two of you there. It warms my heart."

"You aren't jealous he's latched on to me, are you?" Brenda finally opened her eyes and looked at her.

"No," Kay answered with a shake of her head. "It's pretty obvious he loves you as much as I do. It makes me incredibly happy."

"I should be good to go back to my apartment in a few days."

"Is that what you want to do?" Kay kept the smile on her face in spite of the idea frightening her. She liked having Brenda in her life. In her house. She didn't want her to leave but didn't know how to bring up the subject of her possibly moving in. What if Brenda wasn't ready to make a commitment like that?

"No, not really, but I'm sure you'd like to have your house back."

Kay pushed off the doorjamb and walked to the bed. She stretched out next to Brenda and put an arm around her middle, her head on Brenda's shoulder, and held her close, breathing in the clean scent of her shampoo. Her pulse was pounding, but she decided it was time to make the leap.

"Max and I like having you here," she said as if it wasn't obvious. "I'm not sure I'd know what to do with myself if you weren't here anymore."

"What are you saying?"

"How would you feel about moving in with me? Permanently, I mean." Kay held her breath while she waited for an answer, her hand rubbing small circles on Brenda's stomach under her shirt. She was fascinated by the way Brenda's muscles moved under her touch.

"Are you sure you want me here all the time?"

Kay couldn't tell what Brenda was thinking by the tone of her voice, so she lifted her head to look at her. She touched Brenda's cheek and smiled hesitantly.

"If I wasn't sure, I would never have brought it up." Kay kissed her neck before settling in with her head on her shoulder again. "I want you here. I love you, Brenda."

"I love you too," Brenda said with a sigh. Her arm went around Kay's shoulder and she held her closer before kissing the top of her head. "I'd love to move in with you. I have to say, I'm glad we got to know each other so well before we made this leap. I feel good about this."

"Me too." Kay smiled as her hand moved down from Brenda's cheek to her chest. "Not that it was easy keeping my hands to myself for so long, but the end result has been pretty amazing."

"Seriously? Because we met something like two months ago, and we've still only had sex once. You're happy with that?"

"I'm happy with the fact we took our time getting to know each other. And I'm happy we've fallen in love over time, rather than letting everything be muddied up by sex." Kay moved her hand slowly down Brenda's chest and cupped a breast. She smiled when Brenda gasped and leaned into her touch. "And if Rayne hadn't thrown a monkey wrench into our lives, I'm quite certain the vast majority of the past three weeks would have been spent naked in bed. When you're better, we'll have a lot of catching up to do."

"I'm better," Brenda said quietly.

Kay sat up and tucked her legs underneath her as she studied Brenda's face. She'd be lying if she said she hadn't wanted to touch Brenda every night they'd gone to sleep together, but holding her every night was soothing somehow. The first few nights Brenda had awakened in a sweat from a nightmare, but thankfully, those seemed to have stopped now.

"Are you sure?" Kay didn't resist when Brenda took her hand and pulled it back over to her breast. She closed her eyes when she felt the nipple harden under her touch.

"When I saw the doctor yesterday, she said I could resume light physical activity."

"Baby, the physical activity I have planned for you is anything but light." Kay slid her hand under Brenda's T-shirt and found her breast again. When Brenda's hips started a slow thrust, Kay felt herself becoming wet with arousal. "Fuck, Brenda, I'm afraid I'll hurt you."

"I'm better, Kay," she whispered. "I want this. You could never hurt me while you're loving me, I promise."

"You'll tell me if you want me to stop?"

"Yes. Please, just touch me."

Kay moved her hand slowly down her torso and eased under the elastic of Brenda's boxers. When her fingers slid between her legs, Brenda's eyes were hooded with desire and she bit her bottom lip with a groan. Kay's fingers moved easily through her wet and swollen folds before she slipped a finger inside, causing Brenda's hips to buck as her legs fell apart to give her better access.

Max jumped down from the bed after giving Kay a dirty look before going to lie down in the open doorway. His eyes were glued on Brenda, and Kay knew if she did hurt her, Max would come to Brenda's defense.

"Take them off," Brenda pleaded as she tried to push her underwear down her legs. "God, I need to feel your body."

Kay pulled her hand out and removed Brenda's boxers before quickly taking off her own clothes and then Brenda's shirt. A sigh of contentment escaped her when she pressed her naked body against Brenda's.

"You feel amazing," she said into Brenda's ear. When Brenda turned her head to look at her, Kay covered her mouth with her own and jerked her hips when she felt Brenda's tongue against her own.

Brenda moaned into her mouth when Kay put her hand back between her legs and entered her with two fingers. Brenda whimpered before breaking their kiss and moved her hips to match Kay's slow thrusts.

"Baby," she gasped. "You're gonna make me come."

Kay took a nipple between her lips and lightly bit down as her thumb skimmed across Brenda's clit. Brenda's body tensed just when Kay felt the muscles contracting around her fingers, and then Brenda was calling out her name. Brenda held her as her hips bucked wildly, Kay's thumb circling rapidly over her clit, trying to make the orgasm last as long as she possibly could.

"Fuck, fuck, fuck," Brenda said when she reached down to try and still Kay's hand. She opened her eyes and looked at Kay, shaking her head. "Stop, baby, it's too much."

"Too much what?" Kay asked as she slowly pulled her fingers out, relishing the shudder that went through Brenda's body when she did.

"Too intense. I need to just lie here for a minute or two."

"Did I hurt you?"

"No, not at all." Brenda's smile reassured Kay, and she allowed Brenda to guide her head to rest on her chest.

The strong steady beat of her heart under Kay's ear helped to allay any lingering fears she might have had that Tommy Rayne could have taken the most important thing in her life away from her.

With a sigh, Kay knew she was finally right where she was supposed to be, and she intended to stay there for the rest of her life.

About the Author

PJ Trebelhorn was born and raised in the greater metropolitan area of Portland, Oregon. Her love of sports—mainly baseball and ice hockey—was fueled in part by her father's interests. She likes to brag about the fact that her uncle managed the Milwaukee Brewers for five years, and the Chicago Cubs for one year.

PJ now resides in western New York with her partner, Cheryl, their four cats and one very neurotic dog. When not writing or reading, PJ enjoys watching movies, playing on the Playstation, and spending way too much time with stupid games on Facebook. She still roots for the Flyers, Phillies and Eagles, even though she's now in Sabres and Bills territory.

You can write to her at pjtrebelhorn@gmail.com or connect with her on Facebook at www.facebook.com/pjtrebelhorn. You can also check out her website at www.pjtrebelhorn.com.

Books Available from Bold Strokes Books

The Heat of Angels by Lisa Girolami. Fires burn in more than one place in Los Angeles. (978-1-62639-042-3)

Season of the Wolf by Robin Summers. Two women running from their pasts are thrust together by an unimaginable evil. Can they overcome the horrors that haunt them in time to save each other? (978-1-62639-043-0)

Desperate Measures by P. J. Trebelhorn. Homicide detective Kay Griffith and contractor Brenda Jansen meet amidst turmoil neither of them is aware of until murder suspect Tommy Rayne makes his move to exact revenge on Kay. (978-1-62639-044-7)

The Magic Hunt by L.L. Raand. With her Pack being hunted by human extremists and beset by enemies masquerading as friends, can Sylvan protect them and her mate, or will she succumb to the feral rage that threatens to turn her rogue, destroying them all? A Midnight Hunters novel. (978-1-62639-045-4)

Waiting for the Violins by Justine Saracen. After surviving Dunkirk, a scarred and embittered British nurse returns to Nazi-occupied Brussels to join the Resistance, and finds that nothing is fair in love and war. (978-1-62639-046-1)

Because of Her by KE Payne. When Tabby Morton is forced to move to London, she's convinced her life will never be the same again. But the beautiful and intriguing Eden Palmer is about to show her that this time, change is most definitely for the better. (978-1-62639-049-2)

Wingspan by Karis Walsh. Wildlife biologist Bailey Chase is content to live at the wild bird sanctuary she has created on

Washington's Olympic Peninsula until she is lured beyond the safety of isolation by architect Kendall Pearson. (978-1-60282-983-1)

Night Bound by Winter Pennington. Kass struggles to keep her head, her heart, and her relationships in order. She's still having a difficult time accepting being an Alpha female. But her wolf is certain of what she wants and she's intent on securing her power. (978-1-60282-984-8)

Slash and Burn by Valerie Bronwen. The murder of a roundly despised author at an LGBT writer's conference in New Orleans turns Winter Lovelace's relaxing weekend hobnobbing with her peers into a nightmare of suspense—especially when her ex turns up. (978-1-60282-986-2)

The Blush Factor by Gun Brooke. Ice-cold business tycoon Eleanor Ashcroft only cares about the three P's—Power, Profit, and Prosperity—until young Addison Garr makes her doubt both that and the state of her frostbitten heart. (978-1-60282-985-5)

The Quickening: A Sisters of Spirits Novel by Yvonne Heidt. Ghosts, visions, and demons are all in a day's work for Tiffany. But when Kat asks for help on a serial killer case, life takes on another dimension altogether. (978-1-60282-975-6)

Windigo Thrall by Cate Culpepper. Six women trapped in a mountain cabin by a blizzard, stalked by an ancient cannibal demon bent on stealing their sanity—and their lives. (978-1-60282-950-3)

Smoke and Fire by Julie Cannon. Oil and water, passion and desire, a combustible combination. Can two women fight the fire that draws them together and threatens to keep them apart? (978-1-60282-977-0)

Asher's Fault by Elizabeth Wheeler. Fourteen-year-old Asher Price sees the world in black and white, much like the photos he takes, but when his little brother drowns at the same moment Asher experiences his first same-sex kiss, he can no longer hide behind the lens of his camera and eventually discovers he isn't the only one with a secret. (978-1-60282-982-4)

Love and Devotion by Jove Belle. KC Hall trips her way through life, stumbling into an affair with a married bombshell twice her age. Thankfully, her best friend, Emma Reynolds, is there to show her the true meaning of Love and Devotion. (978-1-60282-965-7)

Rush by Carsen Taite. Murder, secrets, and romance combine to create the ultimate rush. (978-1-60282-966-4)

The Shoal of Time by J.M. Redmann. It sounded too easy. Micky Knight is reluctant to take the case because the easy ones often turn into the hard ones, and the hard ones turn into the dangerous ones. In this one, easy turns hard without warning. (978-1-60282-967-1)

In Between by Jane Hoppen. At the age of 14, Sophie Schmidt discovers that she was born an intersexual baby and sets off on a journey to find her place in a world that denies her true existence. (978-1-60282-968-8)

Secret Lies by Amy Dunne. While fleeing from her abuser, Nicola Jackson bumps into Jenny O'Connor, and their unlikely friendship quickly develops into a blossoming romance—but when it comes down to a matter of life or death, are they both willing to face their fears? (978-1-60282-970-1)

Under Her Spell by Maggie Morton. The magic of love brought Terra and Athene together, but now a magical quest stands between them—a quest for Athene's hand in marriage. Will their passion keep them together, or will stronger magic tear them apart? (978-1-60282-973-2)

Homestead by Radclyffe. R. Clayton Sutter figures getting NorthAm Fuel's newest refinery operational on a rolling tract of land in Upstate New York should take a month or two, but then, she hadn't counted on local resistance in the form of vandalism, petitions, and one furious farmer named Tess Rogers. (978-1-60282-956-5)

Battle of Forces: Sera Toujours by Ali Vali. Kendal and Piper return to New Orleans to start the rest of eternity together, but the return of an old enemy makes their peaceful reunion short-lived, especially when they join forces with the new queen of the vampires. (978-1-60282-957-2)

How Sweet It Is by Melissa Brayden. Some things are better than chocolate. Molly O'Brien enjoys her quiet life running the bakeshop in a small town. When the beautiful Jordan Tuscana returns home, Molly can't deny the attraction—or the stirrings of something more. (978-1-60282-958-9)

The Missing Juliet: A Fisher Key Adventure by Sam Cameron. A teenage detective and her friends search for a kidnapped Hollywood star in the Florida Keys. (978-1-60282-959-6)

Amor and More: Love Everafter edited by Radclyffe and Stacia Seaman. Rediscover favorite couples as Bold Strokes Books authors reveal glimpses of life and love beyond the honeymoon in short stories featuring main characters from favorite BSB novels. (978-1-60282-963-3)

First Love by CJ Harte. Finding true love is hard enough, but for Jordan Thompson, daughter of a conservative president, it's challenging, especially when that love is a female rodeo cowgirl. (978-1-60282-949-7)

Pale Wings Protecting by Lesley Davis. Posing as a couple to investigate the abduction of infants, Special Agent Blythe Kent and Detective Daryl Chandler find themselves drawn into a battle over the innocents, with demons on one side and the unlikeliest of protectors on the other. (978-1-60282-964-0)

Mounting Danger by Karis Walsh. Sergeant Rachel Bryce, an outcast on the police force, is put in charge of the department's newly formed mounted division. Can she and polo champion Callan Lanford resist their growing attraction as they struggle to safeguard the disaster-prone unit? (978-1-60282-951-0)

Meeting Chance by Jennifer Lavoie. When man's best friend turns on Aaron Cassidy, the teen keeps his distance until fate puts Chance in his hands. (978-1-60282-952-7)

At Her Feet by Rebekah Weatherspoon. Digital marketing producer Suzanne Kim knows she has found the perfect love in her new mistress Pilar, but before they can make the ultimate commitment, Suzanne's professional life threatens to disrupt their perfectly balanced bliss. (978-1-60282-948-0)

Show of Force by AJ Quinn. A chance meeting between navy pilot Evan Kane and correspondent Tate McKenna takes them on a roller-coaster ride where the stakes are high, but the reward is higher: a chance at love. (978-1-60282-942-8)

Clean Slate by Andrea Bramhall. Can Erin and Morgan work through their individual demons to rediscover their love for each other, or are the unexplainable wounds too deep to heal? (978-1-60282-943-5)

Hold Me Forever by D. Jackson Leigh. An investigation into illegal cloning in the quarter horse racing industry threatens to destroy the growing attraction between Georgia debutante Mae St. John and Louisiana horse trainer Whit Casey. (978-1-60282-944-2)

Trusting Tomorrow by PJ Trebelhorn. Funeral director Logan Swift thinks she's perfectly happy with her solitary life devoted to helping others cope with loss until Brooke Collier moves in next door to care for her elderly grandparents. (978-1-60282-891-9)

Forsaking All Others by Kathleen Knowles. What if what you think you want is the opposite of what makes you happy? (978-1-60282-892-6)

Exit Wounds by VK Powell. When Officer Loane Landry falls in love with ATF informant Abigail Mancuso, she realizes that nothing is as it seems—not the case, not her lover, not even the dead. (978-1-60282-893-3)

Dirty Power by Ashley Bartlett. Cooper's been through hell and back, and she's still broke and on the run. But at least she found the twins. They'll keep her alive. Right? (978-1-60282-896-4)

The Rarest Rose by I. Beacham. After a decade of living in her beloved house, Ele disturbs its past and finds her life being haunted by the presence of a ghost who will show her that true love never dies. (978-1-60282-884-1)

Code of Honor by Radclyffe. The face of terror is hard to recognize—especially when it's homegrown. The next book in the Honor series. (978-1-60282-885-8)

Does She Love You? by Rachel Spangler. When Annabelle and Davis find out they are both in a relationship with the same woman, it leaves them facing life-altering questions about trust, redemption, and the possibility of finding love in the wake of betrayal. (978-1-60282-886-5)

The Road to Her by KE Payne. Sparks fly when actress Holly Croft, star of UK soap Portobello Road, meets her new on-screen love interest, the enigmatic and sexy Elise Manford. (978-1-60282-887-2)

Lightning Source UK Ltd.
Milton Keynes UK
UKHW02f1842140518
322593UK00011B/782/P